Spring of the White Bear

Spring of the White Bear

Anne Robinson

ISBN: 978-1-945247-61-3

Spring of the White Bear

Copyright © 2020 Thurston Howl Publications

First Edition, 2020. All rights reserved.

A Thurston Howl Publications Book

Published by Thurston Howl Publications
thurstonhowlpublications.com
Lansing, MI

cedric.thurstonhowlpub@gmail.com

Cover by Ilya Royz. © 2020
www.artstation.com/Ilyar

Typesetting and design by HYBRID Ink Author Services
www.hybrid.ink

Printed in the United States of America
10 9 8 7 6 5 4 3 2 1

Chapter 1

The bone shaft of Kirima's harpoon flashed white in the afternoon sun. Poised to strike, it reflected the color of the ice as merciless as the spearhead itself.

"Sedna, goddess of the sea, make my aim true," he prayed. "Allow me to take the life of one of your creatures."

With a sudden thrust, the boy drove the head of his spear deep into the skull of the ringed seal. "Success!" cried Kirima in triumph tinged with relief. "This time I did not miss. We will all eat this day!"

Bloody seawater sloshed over the top of the seal's breathing hole in the ice, staining it the color of the spring sunset. Kirima's harpoon line bucked and shivered as the ringed seal fought to escape.

The boy wrapped the line around his left foot to secure the animal while widening the seal's breathing hole with his sharp-edged bone *pana*. With a grunt, he dropped the snow knife and heaved the seal up onto the ice.

Panting with exertion, the boy did not hear the soft scratching of bear claws on the lip of sea ice many sled lengths away.

Screeeee, scrape!

Remaining downwind of its target, the white bear's nose twitched as the beast's claws skittered on the edge of the ice shelf, drawing the bear closer to its target.

The seal attempted to slide back into the water, but Kirima was ready. He grabbed his all-purpose knife from within the top of his sealskin boot. The blade of his *pilaut* ended the seal's struggles. Stepping back, he avoided the gush of blood from the seal's neck that turned the ice to red slush. Kirima sang a prayer of thanks to the seal, setting its soul free to inhabit another seal body and to continue the cycle of life for both seal and the People of the North.

How glad I am to finally bring in a seal! Kirima glanced to the heavens, knowing his father's spirit was nearby. *Father, how proud you would be this day to see your son persevere near the seal's breathing hole, waiting for the perfect moment to strike.*

Screeeee, scrape!

Nanuq pushed off the ice rim and slid low in the water as it slowly approached its target, its black eyes glittering with anticipation of an easy meal.

"Qannik, here!" the boy called as he gutted the seal with his *pilaut*. "Come, Snowflake! See what this strong hunter has caught! Because of my skill, our family and my seal partners will not go hungry this day!"

He held the steaming entrails toward his sled dog. Qannik stretched his nose toward the seal, then lunged at the offering, tail waving in excitement. The odor of fresh meat grabbed the dog's attention, and the prevailing wind carried away the acrid scent of the nearby bear.

Nanuq paddled closer to the seal, its nose homing in on the scent of fresh blood.

"Get back," Kirima said to his dog, gently kneeing him away. "Do not eat more than your share, or we will be in trouble! I am making your load light."

Qannik whined and play bowed, pleading for a bite. Gloves dripping with seal blood, the boy held out a short length of intestine to pacify the dog. Qannik snatched it up and retreated, holding the treat between his forelegs and gulping down large chunks before the snack froze.

"This seal will be a heavy burden to lift into the sled," Kirima mused. "It would easier if I could cut it into smaller pieces." He shook his head. "No," he told his dog. "Grandmother will cut the seal into the right parts. I will not anger the spirits by doing a woman's job."

Screeeee, scrape!

The white bear submerged its body and continued swimming underwater to a closer vantage point.

Kirima took a large bite of the seal's liver to warm himself for the journey home and to pay respect to the sea goddess. His stomach grumbled with hunger, but he restrained himself. The seal's organs, meat and blubber would be shared with Kirima's *nangminarit*. These seal partners, chosen by Kirima's mother when he was still a baby inside her hood, shared in the success of their hunts. Kirima would not eat any meat until all partners had received their portions, but how proud he would be to have something to share.

Screeeee, scrape!

Leaning down, the boy's parka hood flipped down over his forehead as the boy placed the seal innards back inside the body cavity, where they began to freeze to the stomach wall. The seasons were late in turning toward spring, and it was still very cold on the ice shelf. But the sea ice was breaking up; the spirit of the sun was no longer burdened by its winter weight of snow and frost and was able to lift itself into the sky once more.

Kirima wiped his gloves clean on the snow, then cut a slit through the seal's tail fluke, put his knife down on the ice, and tied a short length of caribou sinew through the opening. Grateful for their partnership, he scratched Qannik behind the ears. But when he touched the shallow indentation on the dog's skull—the result of a bully's mean-spirited kick when Qannik was a pup—Kirima frowned. Anger boiled up, but he quickly silenced it. A man did not show emotion, especially on the ice shelf. He had a job to do and could not spend extra energy replaying what was past.

The bear bobbed to the surface; keeping out of sight, it held itself still by hooking its long black claws to the edge of the ice.

Screeeee, scrape!

Nanuq had stalked the boy all afternoon, bobbing just out of sight as the boy sat over the seal's breathing hole. It had seen the boy throw his sealing harpoon earlier, but the spear missed the first seal, glancing off the side of the breathing hole. Now the great bear huffed with impatience. Finally, the seal was there, just out of reach, its body freezing into the bloody slush that gave off such a tantalizing odor.

The white dog whined, begging for more scraps.

Kirima reached out to run his hand affectionately under the jaw of Qannik. "Without a certain white dog," he said, looking into the blue eyes of his companion, "this hunter would not have found the seal. You, Qannik, can sniff out the seal's breathing hole even through a layer of snow."

Screeeee, scrape!

The bear clawed its way out of the sea, water sheeting from its coat. It hid behind a block of ice upthrust by the constant movement of the ocean against the shore. At last, here was the bear's chance!

Kirima looked at the sled and then back at the white dog, wondering if he had the strength to heave the seal into the sled bag. With his back to the white bear, the boy's wide fur hood hid the puffs of breath that floated from the bear's nostrils into the arctic air.

A sudden chill on the back of his neck brought Kirima up short. He glanced about. The victory courted only moments ago slid from his mind and disappeared into the stillness of the late afternoon. The ice shelf was becoming colder by the moment. For the first time since the boy set his harpoon in its rest near the sealing hole, his vulnerability frightened him. He looked down at the *pilaut* still lying on the ice nearby. He was so alone, with only Qannik for company.

The arctic was a dangerous place. Hidden perils lurked around every corner of the sea ice. Shifting ice blocks, an unforeseen break in a snow bridge, a sudden storm that brought white-out conditions—all these could take a man's life as easily as a sharp knife slipped through the ribs of a downed caribou. Was this what his father felt when confronted by the enormity of the empty land?

O Father, if only you could give me courage in this treacherous land.

Kirima was overcome with dread, anxious to leave for home. His attempt to lift the seal into the sled was met by failure as the carcass bounced off the rim of the sled and fell back with a thump onto the ice. Impulsively, the boy fastened the seal directly to Qannik's harness. Qannik wheeled around and tangled his lines, poking the seal with his black nose.

"Get back!" Kirima pulled his dog away from the seal. The dog's jaws snapped only air.

"Leave it alone!" The boy untangled the dog's traces and picked up the sinew tug line attached to the sled. "I am in a hurry; you can pull this heavy seal home. I will pull the sled. You cannot pull both."

Screeeee, scrape!

The bear stood upright on its hind legs, pinpointing the location of its quarry. It lowered itself silently to the ice and advanced on the seal. Its claws caught in a crevice, but it jerked its foot free.

Screeeee, scrape!

Alerting to the sound, Qannik turned, seal meat forgotten. His lips curled upward as he caught the scent of the white bear. He growled a warning deep in this throat.

The bear crouched, putting its paw over its black nose and lay, belly down, on the ice. Then, using its hind feet to propel its body forward, the white bear flowed quietly along the shoreline toward the seal.

Qannik yipped and pulled on his harness. Kirima dropped the tug line of the sled and whipped his head around, tossing back his hood. Catching sight of the approaching bear, which flowed toward the boy on its belly like a malevolent spirit, Kirima's whole body stiffened. The sled's traces dropped soundlessly at his feet.

Nanuq stood, blotting out the sun. Then it growled and lunged toward the seal.

"*Eee-yi!*" the boy cried, lurching backward. His eyes dilated in terror, pupils black against the dark brown of his eyes. Qannik leaped toward the bear, snarling and barking.

"No! Get back!" Kirima yelled. He searched for his knife to cut the dog loose from the seal, but Qannik's wild leaping had kicked it out of reach. Kirima could not catch the flailing lines to release his dog to safety.

Kirima's knees shook and his breath rasped in his throat as his hands began sweating. He was afraid, too afraid to free Qannik from his bloody burden. The bear turned its head as the boy backed slowly away.

The ear! This bear has a mangled ear! Could it be?

Dodging Qannik, the bear pounced. It hooked the seal with its left forepaw. It flung both dog and seal across the sea ice. Qannik regained his feet; despite the weight of the seal, the dog dodged as the bear charged. Catching the bear off guard, Qannik leaped up to bite the stump of the bear's left ear, but the seal's weight jerked him backward. The dog wheeled and leaped again. This time, Qannik bit away the remainder of the ear before letting go. Blood ran down the bear's face, matting a red path in the fur and pooling in its eye.

The bear swiped at the blood with its paw, growling in pain and rage.

"Qannik, come!" shouted Kirima in panic. He inched forward and tried to gather up the traces to pull his dog back, but they slipped out of reach. The boy smelled only the rancid stench of the bear's breath and his own terror. He turned and ran.

Kirima crouched behind an ice block, trembling and panting, his feet slipping on the surface of the ice. He curled into a ball, hiding all but one eye, watching helplessly as his dog launched himself at the white bear again. Howling, Qannik danced around the bear, the seal's carcass skittering behind, as he darted in to grab a mouthful of yellowed fur at the bear's exposed haunch.

With a roar, the bear turned and swiped at Qannik with its forepaw. Qannik dodged the blow and dived at the bear's unprotected side. But again the weight of the seal brought the dog up short. Nanuq's other paw caught Qannik broadside, raking four red lines across the dog's flank. Qannik and the seal skittered across the ice. The dog got up more slowly and stood trembling. The bear lunged at Qannik, roaring.

Whining in pain, Qannik tucked his tail and fled, heading for the distant, rocky shore with the seal bumping along behind him. The bear barged after him, growling and posturing, the massive muscles of its hindquarters bunching and releasing as it pursued its prey.

Kirima put both gloved hands into the space under his armpits to stop their trembling.

"Be still," he told his thumping heart. "Panic on the ice means death."

He stood on wobbly knees and held his hands up to his eyes to focus them in the snow glare as he searched the barren, white landscape. A smear of blood marked the dog's path toward the distant land. The white bear lumbered behind, its paws soundless on the drift snow covering the broken pebbles shingling the beach. The two white figures merged in Kirima's vision as Qannik and the great bear disappeared into the early spring twilight.

"O Father, what do I do now?" Kirima cried.

He lowered his hands. His sled dog was gone. His seal was gone. He was alone. And he was faced with a long trek home, dragging his sled behind him in the rising wind. But worse than all this, his fear had prevented him from cutting the seal away from Qannik. His fear of Nanuq had overshadowed everything.

O Father, how I wish you were here! I should never have tethered the seal to my dog!

"My dog, my white dog!" he cried in agony.

Fighting back tears, the boy picked up his knife and gathered up the rest of his hunting gear, loading it into the sled. He unsnarled the sled's traces and tied them across his chest and over his shoulders. He was reluctant to leave Qannik to the mercy of the white bear, but he had no choice. The bear was too dangerous. He could do nothing now. His dog was gone. It was too late.

With a sob, Kirima leaned into the tug line and began to march back to the seal camp. As he pulled the sled, his eyes returned again and again to the place his dog had vanished, hoping against hope to see Qannik loping back to him. He wiped the tears from his cheeks before they had the chance to freeze and then pounded his fist on the handle of his sled.

"My dog," he cried again. "And the *ear*! Nanuq was missing an ear!"

He kicked the crusty shore ice in sudden anger. Were it not for an earless white bear six winters ago, his father would be beside him, comforting him on his loss and leading the way home. Was it not a father's job to teach his son how to be brave? Was it not a father's job to protect his son against all threats? And yet....

Kirima frowned as the rising wind taunted him with memories of his boyhood. So often he had run to his grandfather for comfort, covering his ears with his small hands, as the hunting party described his father's great failure. But even today, the taunts of the other children still rang in his ears.

The spirit of Nanuq took your father only because he lacked a man's bravery! He cowered before the white bear!

Even now, his father's disgrace shadowed him. And today, the boy experienced again the same feelings of shame and anger that had boiled up in his young chest long ago. Today, his courage had failed. He had run when the bear attacked.

Kirima pulled open the neck of his parka to release the heat of his disgrace into the arctic air. He shook his head to clear his mind from the distant past. Here and now, alone on the ice shelf, was the time to think about the bear of today, so that his mistake would not happen again.

If I had taken time to tie Qaṇnik to the sled and put the seal into the sled basket, all I would have lost this day was the seal.

Kirima groaned with regret. "I was wrong. In my impatience, I heeded the call of my heart, not my head."

Then the boy touched the ptarmigan skull amulet sewn into the lining of his parka hood. "But perhaps I am not to blame. Perhaps it was simple bad luck."

His white dog. As Kirima trudged over the pressure ridge between sea and land, he offered a quick prayer to free Qannik's soul. But memories of the white dog soon overcame him, and Kirima allowed his heart to grieve.

It was in the winter of his eleventh winter that Qannik, still a puppy, had kept Kirima warm under his caribou skins, curled up next to his belly night after night. His parents were adamant that their sled dogs sleep outside, but Kirima could not be dissuaded. Relenting only because the boy was still at the age of indulgence, his parents had insisted that the fluffy white puppy sleep on the very end of the sleeping platform. Qannik would lie down obediently at Kirima's feet, but each night when the snores of the boy's grandfather filled the *iglu*, the mischievous pup would creep up and slide under the caribou skins to rest his black nose on the boy's outstretched arm. There, as the puppy's soft fur warmed the boy's naked chest, Qannik's warm tongue would rasp Kirima's cheek.

When his mother died while giving birth, how Kirima had clung to Qannik's neck, sobbing for his mother and stillborn sister as the puppy squirmed and twisted around to lick away the young boy's tears. In the time to follow, Qannik's puppy antics kept Kirima from falling deep into the abyss of sadness and loss.

The uneven shoreline between the sea ice and the snowy beach broke Kirima's reverie. He stopped and searched in all directions, his heart thudding with the threat of the white bear. Wishing he had not forgotten his snow goggles, he held his hands up to his eyes, shielding them from the late spring sun.

"No bears. I am safe." Speaking the words out loud brought a measure of relief from his fear. His hands had broken out in a sweat again, and he held them in his armpits to allay the bite of the icy wind on his damp skin.

Once again, Kirima stomped his feet and kicked against the crust underfoot. How would he hunt the seal without his Qannik? How would he and his grandfather bring back caribou meat in the summer with only their two remaining dogs?

How would they survive?

As he trudged on, the arctic wind whispered in his grandmother's voice, telling the story of how the sled dog came to live with the People.

"In the beginning," Grandmother had said, "The people who came from the far land that embraces the sun at the end of the day called themselves Chukchi. Through times of plenty, the meat was too heavy for those people to drag back to the seal camp."

While she spoke, Grandmother leaned down from the sleeping platform and used the curved blade of her *ulu* to scratch pictures of the seal hunt in the packed snow of the *iglu* floor.

"Before the dog," she continued, "the women in the camp had to walk to the breathing holes to cut up the seals that the hunters harpooned."

She raised one arm in the air and made a fierce face.

"This was a time of great danger because of Nanuq. The white bear tracked the hunters and stole their seals. Women lost their lives while cutting up meat. And a man without a wife to cook his meat and chew his skins for sewing cannot survive long in this land."

Grandmother showed her teeth, which were worn down to the gums from chewing caribou skins until they were soft enough to work into the family's clothing "Then," she went on, "Sila, the god who breathes life into us all, sent Dog to be their helpers. In time past counting, the Chukchi traveled many seasons to this land, bringing Dog to the People. Our men learned to harness the dogs to haul meat back to the safety of the winter camp. After each hunt, there was dancing and singing, and no one in the village went hungry."

Grandmother flashed her ready smile, holding up her woman's knife. "The dog is as important to the People as the *pana* and the *ulu*."

The memory faded into the wind as Kirima, nearing home at last, made out the curve of his family's *iglu*. Apak, his grandfather, was outside, busy cutting blocks of ice with his snow knife. Nearby, the old man's remaining dogs played together; they would miss Kirima's white dog, just as they had when Grandfather's own favorite dog was lost.

But his grandfather would understand. "There are always other dogs." The boy repeated the words Apak had spoken after the musk ox attack that had taken his own lead dog. "But sometimes there is only one person who can feed the family. Better to sacrifice one's best dog than to risk starvation in the village."

Chapter 2

"And, Apak, guess what? When it stood up, the bear was taller than the snow house! Its roar was louder than a bull walrus at breeding time. And it had only the stump of one ear! Qannik bit the rest of it off!" Kirima held his hands as high as he could, drawing pictures in the air for his grandfather.

His snow knife forgotten, Apak looked at Kirima. Though the old man's eyes were partly concealed in his heavily lined face, the sharpness of his gaze was clear. "One ear?"

Kirima nodded. "One damaged ear."

Apak gazed across the snow blocks to his grandson. "The hunting companions of your father spoke of the damaged ear of the bear that took his life. Perhaps this is the same bear, a bear with a taste for dog and man." His murmur was blown away from Kirima in the freshening wind.

"The bear was after the seal," Kirima said. "And Qannik tried to save me. He tore off the rest of the bear's ear!"

Apak motioned to the boy to come near. He shook his head back and forth, gazing down at Kirima. His grandfather's eyes were kind, the deep color of walrus hide in the early winter. They were wise eyes, far-sighted and understanding. These eyes looked at Kirima now with a hint of sadness in their depths.

Kirima braced himself for what he knew was coming.

Apak resumed his task of cutting blocks with his snow knife. "I see a boy before me who was too lazy to load the seal in the sled and help pull it home," he began. "He was tired and hungry. His head argued with his heart, but his heart whispered in his ear and told him to choose the easy path."

The old man paused to remove his gloves. His gnarled fingers were reddened and frost-scarred from a lifetime of hard work and exposure to the elements. "He may have angered the spirit of the seal by his lack of respect. Instead of losing only a seal to Nanuq, a certain white dog was lost to the great bear as well."

No. Kirima shook his head. *That was not the way it happened. I am not to blame—it was not through my laziness that Qaŋnik was lost to the bear. Bad luck caused the bear to hunt on the same ice shelf.*

Besides, what could a man alone on the ice do to save his dog? Why—had Kirima not hidden himself, he too would be lost to the white bear, and his grandparents would certainly starve. He frowned. *What else could a boy without a father do?*

If only his father had been with him in the flesh and not simply in spirit.

"As a young grandson grows away from boyhood, he will learn to listen to his head and not to his heart," Apak continued. "The hunters who accompanied your father on his last journey said he did not heed the command of his head. His heart stole his courage when the great bear charged, and his companions were too far away to save him. Now my grandson's carelessness has sent another loved one to the spirit world."

Kirima hung his head. The great bear had taken his father's life as easily as the bear of this day had taken Kirima's dog. But the boy could not admit to his grandfather that his fear had eclipsed his good sense. Only small children had the liberty of expressing fear with no consequences—a man did not show his emotions. Besides, it was not his fault.

Kirima pulled out the neck of his parka in frustration.

"It was bad luck!"

"There is no luck," Apak said sternly. "The People make their own fortune and do not tempt the spirits."

It was a knife in his heart to hear harsh words from this gentle, kind-hearted man. Kirima lowered his eyes, rebellion smoldering in their depths. He did not want to show his hurt to the man who had fed and educated him after his father joined the spirit world. What could he say to redeem himself?

"When the bear chased Qannik down the beach," Kirima said, "this hunter remembered a truth. It is better to lose even the best dog than risk starvation."

Apak grunted, piling a third row of blocks atop the second, forming the beginnings of a new windbreak for the sled dogs. He shoved a piece of caribou antler into a crack between the blocks. "Losing a friend by one's own hand can cut the spirit like the edge of a *pana*." Apak's eyes held a sudden compassion. "Life is often unkind for both dog and man. My grandson escaped the bear. Yes—it is better for a man to lose his dog than his life."

A man. Grandfather had called him a man! A rush of warmth filled Kirima's chest as a small smile crept onto his face. The boy did not dare tell Apak about his shout of triumph at the seal's capture or his moment of panic when the bear attacked. Bad enough that he had lost Qannik. He did not want the old man to know that he had slipped from manhood back into childhood with his boasting and trembling. But Kirima was called a man!

The boy reached inside his parka to grasp his ptarmigan skull amulet. Given to him when he killed his first seal, this amulet was very old and therefore very powerful, having gained spiritual strength over time. The spirit housed within the ptarmigan skull was tasked with protecting Kirima and ensuring that Kirima became a *real* man, endowed with strength both of body and character.

Kirima caressed the skull through the heavy caribou hide of his parka hood. *This man thinks that his amulet's spirit looked away when he bragged to Qannik, and then looked back just in time to spare this unlucky hunter's life.* Even in his thoughts, Kirima was careful to use the formal language of respect to appease any evil spirits that might be hovering nearby. He cast his eyes downward. *Perhaps the amulet's spirit looked away so it would not see my fear.*

Kirima turned toward his grandfather's snow house, hiding the shame of his fear from Apak. To deflect his emotions, he called out to the family's remaining sled dogs. He dug into his sled bag and pulled out several lake trout. He tossed one to each dog, smiling sadly at their antics as they leaped and twisted to catch the treats mid-air. How he wished his white dog was there to tease Gray Dog out of his meal; how he wished to see Qannik crouch in deference to his red mother.

Then the boy returned to help his grandfather heave the final snow block onto the wall.

Apak's breath came out in short gasps as he groaned with the effort of placing the last block. Kirima passed his snow knife between the block joints, softening the snow enough to make a strong seal.

"The Soul of the North smiled on you today," Apak said in his gravelly voice. "Not many People who find themselves close to such a bear would live to tell the story. An old man thinks that this bear may be the same one that took the spirit of his own son."

Kirima shuddered at the older man's words. Until he himself had faced the bear's sudden roar, its acrid scent, and the power of its claws, Kirima had not truly appreciated the horror of his father's death. A shiver slashed its way down his back, and the boy quickly jabbed his knife between two snow blocks to hide his shuddering.

"Why does the white bear hunt men, Apak?" he asked, wielding his *pana* with dexterity between the snow blocks, chiseling away the spaces between them.

"The blood of the People is brother to the sea," Apak answered. "A bear needs salt to keep its blood from freezing in the dark season. That is why a bear will eat a man and at times will even hunt for him."

Kirima's lips drew back in distaste, remembering the smell of the bear's grimy fur and the sharp curve of its yellow teeth. Replacing his *pana* in the top of his boot, he began to move past his grandfather and toward the tunnel leading into the snow house.

Apak nodded. "There. Now that the season of the wind is changing, this new windbreak will keep the dogs comfortable during a storm." Then he indicated the snow shovel at his feet. "It would be helpful if someone were to throw snow on this wall to seal the blocks."

"Women and children are useful for this task," Kirima answered. "They do this job well."

Grandfather gave Kirima a pointed look and gestured again toward the wall. The boy sighed and took up the shovel—a flat piece of caribou scapula lashed to a caribou femur bone. Throwing the fur-lined hood off his face, he tossed several shovelfuls of snow on the block wall, filling the gaps between the blocks. *Did not Apak call me a man? I can kill a seal like a man, accept loss like a man, and keep my feelings hidden. I have sixteen winters, yet I am treated like a boy.* Kirima hid a grimace.

As the boy completed the job, Apak gathered up the dogs and tethered them to the caribou antler, now frozen firmly into the side of the windbreak. Kirima stowed the snow shovel beside the *iglu*, picked up his sealing harpoon, and followed his grandfather into the tunnel of their winter home. Kirima grunted as he crawled through the narrow channel, trying to keep his head from hitting the roof. His harpoon snicked against the walls of the tunnel, flaking white powder underfoot.

Kirima resembled the typical Inuk with even features and smooth skin. Under his fur-lined hood, Kirima's hair was black and coarse, tied back with caribou sinew and glistening with a film of seal fat. Above an aquiline nose, his black eyes were lively with a ready glint of mischief. His cheeks were still full, even though the fish and caribou stores rotting into sweetness inside the family's meat cache had dwindled to almost nothing.

By the time Kirima reached the entry porch inside the snow house, his clothes had picked up a fine layer of ice from the sides of the tunnel. His eyes adjusted quickly to the low light as he set his harpoon aside and reached for a flat piece of driftwood. He handed this to his grandfather so that the older man could beat his own clothes free of ice. Though arctic air filled the tunnel, its downward slope trapped the cold before it could enter their dwelling. If the snow on their outer clothing melted in the warmth of the *iglu* and then re-froze overnight, it would be impossible to dress in the morning. Then his grandmother would need to spend long moments chewing the skins to softness again.

"*Eee-yi!*" A voice floated out from the sleeping platform as Kirima's grandmother raised her eyes from the garment she was sewing. She showed a gummy smile. "Did my fierce wall-builder and his grandson remember to beat the snow off their clothing?" she asked. "An old woman's teeth are working hard enough!"

"Yes, Grandmother," Kirima said.

"Our clothes are dry," Grandfather answered, his mouth keeping a ready smile hidden just beneath the surface. Then, revealing his own two missing front teeth, he continued, "Your teeth are safe!"

Kirima nodded, "Grandmother, I met a white bear on the ice shelf! Qannik saved my life!" He hoped that his grandmother at least would see his tragedy in a different light. "We were attacked by Nanuq, and Qannik took the bear away."

"Attacked?" Grandmother set down the bird skin shirt and needle. Her shrewd eyes looked Kirima up and down. "Is this young hunter certain that the bear attacked both the boy and the dog?"

"The bear attacked the seal this hunter caught. The dog attacked the bear," Kirima clarified his earlier statement. "Qannik led the bear away, but he is gone, too. The bear...the bear was too powerful."

"A brave dog will defend his master to the death. This old woman grieves for his loss." With her bone needle, Grandmother pointed to Kirima's sealing spear. "And did my grandson bring back the seal? There is talk in the village that the spirits are angry and seals are disappearing from the winter camp."

Before Kirima could answer, Grandmother held up her hand, stopping him at the snow house entrance. She spoke again, gesturing to the layer of unmarked snow at her feet. "Do not walk on the *iglu* floor! This old woman has put down fresh snow in the seal's honor and will not anger the seal's spirit by butchering on a dirty floor."

Kirima sighed. "The spirits looked away, and I could not cut Qannik away from the seal in time," he said. "The bear took the seal, too."

"These dim eyes see a hunter who is fortunate," Grandmother answered gently. "He is home alive with only the loss of a seal and a dog to remember this day. That dog will be missed." She gestured toward the heart of the home—the soapstone lamp flickering below. "Come and put the harpoon head that killed the seal here. The seal's spirit still lives in the tip, even though its body is dancing with a white dog."

Stepping up to the cooking area of the snow house, Kirima placed the harpoon head as well as the shaft and line next to the soapstone lamp. There it would remain throughout the night, warming the spirit of the seal and placating it for the sudden loss of its body.

Then Kirima undressed and laid his outer garments on the drying net above the cooking frame. Using his teeth, he removed his mittens and set them to dry over the ends of the caribou antlers frozen into the side of the *iglu* wall.

In her kindness, Kirima's grandmother had made the loss of the seal less important than the loss of the dog. But the boy knew that his grandfather depended upon him more and more to provide for the family. The old man had not the stamina to spend a long time at a breathing hole, nor had he the strength to bring home a fully grown seal by himself. Without the seals and fish the boy brought back, neither their seal partners nor Kirima's uncles could sustain the family for long. Food was scarce enough in good times; in lean times, there was not enough to share. Kirima had seen the prominent ribs of most of the village's sled dogs, had heard children crying in hunger in the night. The entire village hovered on the brink of starvation. The seals were no longer plentiful at the winter camp, and the one he lost today had cost his village dearly.

"Good fortune has found its way to this family's cooking pot," Grandmother continued, smiling at her grandson. "Your *sennerak* has brought back a seal, his first in many sleeps. I will prepare our cooking pot to accept the seal meat for tonight. Go now and stuff your boots with new grasses. You will find Tulimaq in his snow house. His wife has prepared this family's share."

As with Kirima's other seal partners, his mother had chosen Tulimaq, the boy's side partner, long ago. As Tulimaq's *sennerak*, Kirima received the long piece of meat from the side of the seal's abdomen, along with some of the blubber. This sharing system assured that all members of the various seal partnerships had meat in the cooking pot, no matter the outcome of each individual hunt.

Kirima sighed with relief. Tonight, his family would have food to eat and blubber to keep his grandmother's soapstone lamp burning.

Kirima bowed his head. "This boy thanks Tatqeq for Tulimaq's luck and protection against the evil spirits. They have only taken Qannik this day and not the *sennerak's* seal," he murmured.

Grandmother smiled. "Be sure Tatqeq is thanked only for protecting you," she said, laughing. "The moon spirit brings more than luck—he must not think he is also to send this *iglu* more mouths to feed."

Kirima laughed quietly, understanding. "No more mouths," he promised.

Kirima sang a song of thanks to Tatqeq as he gathered up his outer garments. He removed his boots and re-dressed himself with the fur side of his caribou parka facing outward in order to trap as much warm air as possible. Then, for extra insulation, the boy pulled a few handfuls of dried grass from his grandmother's supply. He shoved the grass between the soles of his hare skin stockings and his outer sealskin boots.

"Give me the boots from your feet when you return," Grandmother told him. "An old woman with short teeth will keep them in her sleeping skins overnight. Someone's grandmother has seen that when a certain boy's boots sleep with him on this platform, she has to do a lot of chewing in the morning!"

Kirima nodded at Grandmother as she once again took up her needle and his grandfather's new bird skin shirt. As always when sewing, she sat against the back wall of the sleeping platform with legs straight in front of her, her gray hair tied neatly at the back of her deeply lined neck. She hummed to herself as she bent over the yellow skins. Taking almost invisible stitches with her needle and sinew thread, she sewed the individual pieces until they looked as if they had grown together.

Kirima walked toward his seal partner's snow house, boots squeaking on the dry snow. Tulimaq, too, was busy building a windbreak for his team of sled dogs. He stopped working when the boy approached.

"Where is Qannik?" Tulimaq asked. "Village talk is as swift as a stampeding caribou. Many people saw my side partner came off the ice without his dog."

"White bear," Kirima said tersely. "It took the seal, too."

"Ah, pah," was Tulimaq's answer. "This is a big loss. That dog could find a breathing hole in a winter snowstorm. Too bad you did not take those fox skins for him last summer when Yutu offered. But one less dog to feed, eh?"

"Yutu—pah!" Kirima's lip curled at the bully's name, just as Qannik's lip had lifted into a snarl whenever Yutu came near. Coughing to dispel his tension, Kirima told Tulimaq, "I would rather see Qannik dancing in the Sky Village than pulling that boy's sled."

"Yutu may have spent too much time in his mother's hood," said Tulimaq, "but he is not as spoiled as in seasons past. And he is learning to hunt for his family."

"Perhaps this is so," Kirima responded grudgingly, although his heart said otherwise. "But the broken-toothed one will never be included in my hunts. I have no wish to associate with Yutu."

"This wall is finished just in time," Kirima's seal partner said as he placed the final block. "There is a great wind building." Tulimaq handed Kirima a snow shovel and gestured toward the windward side of the wall. "Pack the cracks between these snow blocks. Then go collect the seal meat."

The boy hesitated before throwing snow on the blocks. *Everyone treats me like a child!*

Then, to Kirima's surprise, Tulimaq picked up a second shovel and worked on the opposite side of the windbreak. Their task completed in half the usual time, Kirima ducked into Tulimaq's snow house, the older man right behind.

"It is an honor to share with a seal partner." Liak, Tulimaq's wife, arose from her work of butchering the seal. She took a wrapped package from a cavity dug into the side of the *iglu* wall, and eyes politely downcast, handed it to Kirima. "Please give this unworthy woman's greatest respects to your grandparents."

Kirima bowed gracefully in thanks, accepting the package of seal meat from Liak's outstretched hands. As their hands touched, Kirima's heart fluttered in his chest, and his stomach seemed to drop to the *iglu* floor. Surprised at his extraordinary response, he backed away and turned to Tulimaq in confusion. The older man had paused at the snow house entrance and was beating the snow from his jacket.

"Tell, uh...tell about your, uh, your hunt, Tulimaq," the boy stuttered, glancing back at Liak. He was relieved to find her head bowed, eyes downcast with her long eyelashes dark against her cheeks. "Did...did the seal fight hard?"

Tulimaq answered with ritual modesty. "Oh, it was nothing. This hunter was clumsy, and the seal did him a favor by letting the harpoon pierce its head." He gestured toward the remainder of the seal. "Look at it! As small as a newborn walrus floating on its mother's back!"

Liak looked up. "My husband will not offend the spirits by boasting," she said. "But I can tell you that the seal fought hard and was heavy even for the strong hunter of this snow house."

"I remember your first seal, Kirima," Tulimaq said. "It was not long after your father's death. You sat all day at that seal's breathing hole until the arm that held your seal hook was trembling." Tulimaq held up his arm, making it quiver in the soft light. "And when you finally caught the seal, you were so tired you almost fell into the breathing hole! Now that was a big seal."

"I remember it well," Kirima said, sneaking a glance at Tulimaq's wife. "And my *sennerak* stepped into my father's place and helped me land that seal. I still thank you for not mentioning this at the drum dance."

"Some day when you find yourself again at this hearth, I will tell you another story. The drum dance honoring my first seal was very different from yours. My father traded kindness for laughter, and your seal partner was embarrassed for days afterward."

Kirima tore his eyes away from Liak's hands, which were busy adjusting the flame under her cooking pot. He shook his head to dispel the image and turned his attention back to Tulimaq. "I...I will look forward to your story."

The angry sputter of the soapstone lamp brought forth an echoing sputter of frustration from Liak. "A seal has given itself to us today," she said, adjusting the moss wick again. Karima found himself admiring the shadow the woman's graceful form cast upon the *iglu* wall. Tulimaq's wife looked at the hunters as she continued. "The villagers will not go to sleep tonight in fear of the starving time."

"Yes, perhaps not all the seals have deserted the People," Kirima agreed. Although he stood in the familiar snow house of his side partner, his confusion and disorientation persisted. He coughed to hide his bewilderment. Liak had always been simply Liak, his seal partner's wife. But today he saw her differently as a completely new sensation rose in his chest.

What is happening to my stomach? And why is Liak suddenly more fascinating than she has ever been?

Folding his arms across his body, Tulimaq broke into the boy's reverie. "The bowhead whale and the walrus have abandoned their feeding grounds. Now the ringed seals are vanishing. The hunters do not find many breathing holes, and even the white bears walk with empty bellies and sagging skin."

"Yes, we must take extra care to guard the spirits of the ringed seal," said

Kirima, suddenly alert. "If the seals follow the whale to other oceans, we all will starve."

Liak cleared her throat and smiled. "Kirima, take your seal portion home now. Your grandmother's stomach is waiting."

The turmoil returned to Kirima's stomach as he noticed the dimples in Liak's cheeks. Still, he glimpsed the worry in her eyes before she turned her head away from the seal partners.

Nodding in thanks, the boy tucked the parcel of seal meat under his parka and hurried out into the rising wind. Relieved to be away from the distraction of the two lively indentations on either side of Liak's smiling mouth, he pondered the mystery of his new, unbidden feelings toward her.

Kirima whispered so softly that only he heard the words. "My stomach turned over like it does when a hunting party sings out across the sea after sighting a whale. It felt like it does when the dogs pull the sled over the lip of a sharp hill. Is this what Grandmother calls 'spirit-to-spirit talk'?"

As he neared his snow house, the voices of his grandfather's two dogs *woo-wooed* in welcome. A sharp pain replaced the confusion in Kirima's heart. The absence of a special dog's voice reminded him of his loss. Never before had Qannik's place alongside the other dogs looked so empty. The boy had known hurt at the loss of his mother and father, but never had the boy's heart hurt in this particular way.

In the shock of the bear attack, Kirima had offered only a rushed prayer to free Qannik's soul when the dog was lost. The boy now had time to compose a more meaningful prayer for the rapid release of Qannik's spirit into the Great Beyond. Even a devoted sled dog could return in spirit to do harm to the village if his soul was unhappy in the afterlife.

Go, white dog, run fast!
Run to the sea

Run to the sky
Run to the wind
Your time is now
Your time is ever
You are all time
All sea
All sky

Kirima touched his ptarmigan amulet as he looked toward the heavens. Had he done enough to send Qannik to the spirit world? Was Qannik's soul joyful tonight as the dog romped with fallen comrades, both canine and human, while the goddess Tapasuma smiled upon them?

I wonder if the souls of my father and my white dog have met in the Great Sky Village.

Kirima blinked back tears to think of his father and Qannik vanishing into the whiteness of the frozen north. If only Tapasuma would send him a sign that his dog and father were united in peace and love in the land of perpetual daylight.

Kirima's footsteps slowed as he allowed himself to remember the rituals observed after his father's disappearance. The spirit of his father was certain to have been angry at his sudden departure from the Earth. To worsen matters, his bones could not be found and thus could not rest in an ice grave. Fearing the wrath of his spirit, the villagers complied diligently with all the rules of the mourning period. For five days, all work had ceased for the immediate family as his father's soul left his body and traveled to the land of perpetual daylight. The villagers took turns bringing food to Kirima and his grandparents, and one of his grandmother's cousins came each day to chew their boots to softness. Thus his father's spirit was soothed; no calamities had stricken the village after his death.

Shaking off his sadness, Kirima approached his winter home. As he squeaked through the dry snow, a great commotion arose from the seal camp. Dogs howled and pulled at their tethers. Children ran, shouted, and pointed toward the tundra. Villagers streamed from their *iglus* and began to run toward the center of the winter camp.

What is happening? Kirima drew in a sharp breath.

A great wind began to build; its sound was unlike that heard by even the most seasoned ears. It was as though all the animals on the land and the sea began to howl in unison. The boy frowned as he scanned the landscape, trying to find the direction of the sound. But the wind moaned eerily, seeming to echo from all directions at once.

Through the blowing snow, Kirima made out a distant shape drawing toward the encampment. Four black dogs, fan-hitched in a semicircle, emerged through the white curtain to gallop toward the village. Their tails were erect and stiff with tension, and the whites of their eyes gleamed against their dark fur. An imposing figure sat in the sled basket, his back straight and his head turned toward the camp. Behind the sled basket, a smaller figure hunched over the crossbar as he clung to the sled handle.

The wind did not increase in strength, but it increased in pitch. It shrieked and howled like a pack of wolves driven mad by hunger. It roared and rumbled like a bull walrus when a hunter's spear inflicts a mortal wound. It made Kirima's ears ring and his hair stand on end. His heart contracted with fear as the wind swept through the seal camp.

Has this fearsome wind brought an evil spirit? Why does it behave unlike any other wind that comes here unbidden—what is happening?

As the entire village scurried from their snow houses, they began to cry out. "Angakok! The wind has brought Angakok to us!"

Kirima gasped. The shaman! He had come from the land of thunder and snow. He had come from the place where the spirits dwelled and the seal and caribou took human form.

Hastily, Kirima dumped the side portion of his seal next to the wall of his family's snow house. Bending forward into the swirling wind, he hurried with the rest of the villagers toward the center of the camp to meet the spiritual leader. Not every day, or even every season, did the shaman come to the People.

Chapter 3

Still clinging to the sled handle, Angakok's companion turned the sled toward a large snow house in the middle of the settlement. Unlike the other *iglus*, this meeting house had no sleeping platform or cooking hearth. A smaller structure for these purposes adjoined the building, for the snow house itself was a gathering place.

The drum dance for the Return of the Sun had taken place here almost two moons ago. Here, too, festivals celebrated successful seal hunts. And when the People gathered in this snow house to reinforce their alliances, spontaneous song fellowships frequently broke out amid much joking and laughter. But Kirima did not anticipate merriment in the meeting house today. Although the boy had never seen the shaman before, he knew Angakok's visit was serious.

As Kirima drew closer, the shaman's helper halted the dog team and set his snow hook. As if on cue, the howling wind accentuating the shaman's sudden appearance dropped to a whisper.

Kirima halted outside the meeting house, alarmed at the eerie silence that had descended over the camp. *Now what is happening?*

"An old woman is lucky to have found the side meat and begun its preparation before the dogs did." Grandmother's words drifted toward the boy through the early evening gloom. "This young hunter did not take time to cache the seal as he should. And an old man and his grandson are lucky that the cooking pot and not the dogs' stomachs cradle the seal meat this evening."

Kirima ducked his head, partly in apology and partly to hide his concern over the mysterious wind.

"The pot is now simmering in gratitude," said his grandmother.

"You would have been better served to bring the side of seal into the snow house," Grandfather scolded Kirima as he joined them. "The dogs have eaten for the day."

Kirima bobbed his head again, casting down his eyes as his face warmed. Shame tinged with impatience rose in his chest.

"The shaman's sudden appearance made me act in haste. It is not my fault!"

The whine of the black dogs turned Kirima's attention back to the holy man's sled. The shaman melted into the twilight, disappearing behind the large snow house. Kirima shivered as the other villagers followed Angakok into the meeting hall.

"Apak," he said, trying hard to keep a twinge of fear from his voice. "The...the wind?"

"The Great Wind brings Angakok to the People. He cannot travel without it," Grandfather's reply was matter-of-fact. He placed a reassuring hand on his grandson's shoulder.

Kirima's shoulders relaxed. Then an evil spirit had not visited the camp. He sighed in relief and stepped back to allow his grandparents to enter the meeting hall before him.

His grandmother's stomach gave a loud growl.

Apak turned to his wife with a sudden smile. "Even a meeting with the shaman will not silence a grandmother's demanding gut."

"Hush, old man," Grandmother replied. "Do you not see this woman walking to the meeting hall alongside her husband instead of tending the flame underneath the cooking skin?"

Though not all villagers were present, those who were filled the large snow house with noise and turmoil as they assembled. A storm of emotions whirled around the hall as voices flew back and forth in the close space. To make room, fathers, brothers, and uncles picked up the youngest children and held them on their shoulders. Babies still in their mothers' hoods squirmed and stared at the gathered villagers. The hubbub added to the excitement building in Kirima's chest.

The frozen walls of the icehouse glistened as the heat from the assembled camp softened the icy enclosure. One of the village men took his *pana* and carved several small ventilation holes into the walls, letting in the frigid air. The slush refroze, further insulating the large *iglu* from the outside cold.

A sudden movement across the room caught Kirima's eye. A stocky boy in a caribou parka lined with wolverine fur slid a piece of antler out of his coat. He tested its tines for sharpness before then hiding the antler behind his back. An evil smile revealed his broken teeth, transforming the boy's face.

Kirima's heart leaped. "Yutu, *no!*"

But his voice was lost in the villagers' excited chatter. Kirima began to push through the crowd toward Yutu, his eyes scanning the crowd in hopes that the bully's parents would intervene.

Yutu turned his back on the villagers, blocking their sight as he approached a group of young boys. Then he jabbed the antler toward the exposed neck of the smallest boy. "The caribou gores the frightened lemming!"

The boy jumped away, stumbling over his feet in the crowded hall.

Yutu smiled with pleasure. Still forcing his way through the crowd, Kirima shouted again as the bully lifted his booted foot and kicked at the ankles of the youngster. Arms windmilling to keep his balance, the boy fell sideways, collapsing against the wall. He landed hard on his shoulder.

Yutu laughed aloud and gestured to the boy. "Clumsy fool!" Yutu hissed. "You belong out on the ice with the old ones!"

The nearby villagers turned as Yutu's voice rang out. Before they could react, though, Kirima squirmed free of the throng and confronted Yutu, his eyes narrowed and his heart pounding.

"Leave him be, Yutu," said Kirima, his voice deepening in anger. "There is no glory in taunting children." He helped the boy up, moving him protectively behind his own body, and the other youngsters took shelter behind him as well.

Several men of the winter camp now surrounded the group, crossing their arms and frowning as they observed the confrontation. But they would only interfere if Kirima's or Yutu's anger spilled beyond what was tolerated by villagers.

Yutu ignored the village men and spoke only to Kirima. "Should this powerful caribou taunt you, then? You go out on the hunt alone and think that you are no longer a child! I hear you came off the ice without your best dog today! Did you lose him the same way your father lost his life?"

Then, elbowing the younger boys out of his way, the bully jabbed Kirima with the antler. "Coward! You were a coward! A coward and a child! You even have the name of a girl!"

Kirima wanted to leap at Yutu and pound him into the packed ice of the meeting hall floor. The bully's words cut deeply, but Kirima knew he must curb his building anger. He could not risk allowing Yutu to provoke him into action. He took a deep breath, holding onto the hem of his parka to silence his hands.

"My name honors the great-grandmother of my father's hearth," said Kirima, his upper lip curling with enmity. "Even you should know that this hunter wears the name with a man's pride."

Yutu snarled, curling his own lips and jabbing the antler at Kirima again. "You are not a man!"

Kirima lowered his voice once again, purposefully using the I pronoun emphatically to express his anger. "I am who I am, no matter what the name. I do not lower myself by hurting small children and kicking defenseless puppies."

Enraged now, Yutu dropped the antler and made a fist, cocking his arm backward. Kirima crouched, ready to defend himself.

"Qannik deserved it!" Yutu cried. "He ran under my feet and deserved more than just a kick!"

The surrounding men began to grumble with disapproval as they uncrossed their arms.

Suddenly, Kirima did not care about the customs of the People. He clenched his fists. *If Yutu swings his fist at me, I will flatten him like the sled runner flattens the late spring ice crust.*

"Stop!" Tulimaq's loud voice interrupted the two contenders. "This man sees two boys whose time to act like children passed long ago."

Kirima's seal partner placed himself between the two boys. "Kirima, your grandfather awaits your company. Yutu, your mother spoils her son as the summer sun spoils fish left too long on the riverbank. Your anger conquers your good sense. It is best that you leave the hall and go home to your parents."

Yutu cocked his fist at the older man with false bravado. Tulimaq took a step toward the boy, and Yutu turned pale, tripping back out of reach.

"Go now," Tulimaq said quietly.

With a sideways glance at Kirima, Yutu stumbled from the meeting hall, grumbling under his breath.

Kirima watched him go, heart pounding, torn between relief and disappointment. *How dare Yutu call me a child! I hope he thinks I just showed the patience of a man by restraining myself.* Kirima sighed, unclenching his fists. *I am glad my* sennerak *intervened before I lost control and started to fight as I would have when I was a child.*

Suddenly, a hush fell over the crowd. All heads turned toward the back of the large room.

Angakok emerged from the rear sleeping chamber, striding into the assembly. Above his aquiline nose, his eyes shone fiercely, glinting in the dark of the meeting hall, penetrating to the very end of the hall itself. The shaman's assistant slunk in behind him, making himself as unobtrusive as possible. He took his place near the bear hide that covered the doorway to the sleeping area.

The crowd parted to allow the shaman to pass. Angakok stopped in the middle of the dancing area. The villagers gathered around, wide-eyed with curiosity. As Kirima watched, Angakok's stature grew until the spellbound boy believed the shaman towered above the crowd.

"The starving time is upon us!" The shaman's voice resonated in the enclosed space. "This is not the starving time of days or moons or even seasons. This is a starving time that may end the People's time on Earth."

Fear leaped across the faces of everyone in the congregation.

"Angakok has traveled with Kinak, god of the north winds, and has looked down upon the land," the shaman went on. "He has seen a sight beyond all imagining. A tall wooden *umiak* sits frozen in the sea beyond the pack ice. This *umiak* is larger than the house for the drum dance, larger even than the entire winter seal camp."

A murmur of amazement greeted this pronouncement.

"This wooden *umiak* has many tall antlers hung taut with white skins. The antlers come from giant caribou, many people high," the shaman continued. "In his dream, Angakok has seen people walking upon the top of *umiak.*"

"Why have these people come to our sea?" Kirima's grandfather called out.

"Your shaman is searching for the answer," answered Angakok. "He believes the spirits of the Great Cold may have brought this vessel to the village. He believes a new race of people, the Kabloonas, have come to do us harm and block the walrus and seals from coming to our land."

The shaman paused as a low murmur arose from the crowd, slowly building to a crescendo. Some of the older villagers cried out with alarm. A few of the women hid their faces in the hoods of their parkas. Most of the adults quickly reached inside their parkas to touch their amulets. A low moan filled the room as the wind began to growl again, overpowering the clamor of the crowd.

"What is the Great Cold?" Kirima whispered to his grandfather, dread touching his heart.

"The Great Cold took place long before your spirit came down from the Sky Village to dwell upon this Earth," Apak answered. "The sea goddess became angry and sent us seasons with no summer. The bowhead whales disappeared. The Inuit were forced to abandon their permanent villages under the Fixed Star and wander in search of the great whale."

Apak paused, deep in reverie. Then he continued. "Our People moved to this land, but even here, the whales that sustained the People for time beyond counting had vanished. We relied on the ringed seal to sustain us, and we honored the seal by calling ourselves Netsilik. That is why this village hunts the ringed seal and walrus in winter and the caribou in summer."

"This is true. We find no whales to hunt. Now the seals are leaving this land, too," Kirima whispered. "If they disappear, we will no longer call ourselves Netsilik, People of the Seal."

Kirima's grandfather shook his head in sadness as the shaman held up his arms for quiet, his sleeves falling back to his elbows.

"Shhhh," Apak whispered. "Let lips close and ears open."

The shaman's voice boomed forth over the wind once more. "Taboos have been broken, and the spirits of the Great Cold may have released some evil spirit residing in the great *umiak*. Angakok will send his spirit on a journey to the place where the sea meets the summer sun. On this vision quest, his spirit will speak to the spirits of the great boat to determine what the People must do to placate the evil that has come upon us."

The crowd began to murmur again and stamped their feet, creating a sound like the hooves of a herd of migrating caribou. Many coughed to relieve their anxiety.

The shaman's fierce eyes scanned the restless crowd as if searching for someone. When Angakok's gaze skimmed over Kirima, the boy shrank against his grandfather in fear. Others averted their eyes as well as the shaman studied the villagers several more times. Then the holy man's gaze returned to Kirima.

The wind subsided abruptly as the shaman looked deeply into the boy's eyes, nodding slowly as if a decision had been made. Try as he might, Kirima could not break free of the shaman's gaze. Then, as if echoing the sudden near-silence of the wind, the shaman's voice dropped to a whisper.

"You will be chosen."

Angakok slapped his palms to his chest and wheeled around, the hood of his parka twirling out from his neck. Then he strode back through the doorway into the rear chamber. His small, twisted aide shuffled after the holy man and lowered the bearskin across the entry for privacy. The meeting was over.

The villagers exited the hall, murmuring in consternation. Still at Apak's side, Kirima stood transfixed while the others flowed around him as the summer tide eddies around the boulders that litter the beach.

Did he mean me? Did Angakok really look at me?

A familiar voice, together with an affectionate slap on the boy's back, brought Kirima back to reality.

"A great *umiak*!" The jolly face of Akkak, Kirima's uncle, grinned up at the boy. Then he turned to Apak. "Did Angakok not say it is made from wood?"

Still immobile, Kirima stared at Akkak. *Did no one notice the shaman point to me with his eyes? Was I the only one who saw this?*

Now the three joined the exodus from the meeting hall. "Yes, son, it is wood," answered Apak. "This old man has never seen such a thing, though he hears that toward the southern sky are stands of wood called forest. This forest reaches toward the clouds and holds up its arms like little children. The tribes who dwell there use the forest to build their homes. This man has heard it said that there is enough wood to build all the houses in their village."

"But the People have wood also," Akkak said. "Are not this village's summer tent frames built with summer wood?"

Apak shook his head. "This old man is talking about wood that has not been shaped by the sea and cast upon the shore. I have heard that these wooden houses can withstand even the great winds from the North."

Momentarily forgetting his confusion over Angakok's visit, Kirima gasped, unable to imagine such tall stands of wood.

"This great *umiak*," Akkak brought himself to a halt, his short legs sliding a bit on the frozen ground. "How did it come to rest on the shores of the Netsilik? Did spirit women paddle it to our lands?"

"This is a great mystery, my son," Grandfather answered. "Let patience visit the seal camp. In time, we will see what the shaman's dream reveals."

With a gesture of greeting to Akkak, Grandmother joined the men. Her stomach gave another rumble of hunger under her caribou skin parka.

"Go home now to your wife, my son," she said to Akkak. "Let our six feet find their way home to stand before the cooking pot. Tulimaq's seal should be ready."

"Old woman, your stomach rules a husband's days," Apak said, smiling as they parted with Akkak and turned toward their own *iglu*. Kirima trudged behind, hoping for an opening to give voice to what he thought had transpired in the meeting hall.

"This stomach keeps a family fed," Grandmother retorted. "Without this woman's butchering and cooking, two fierce wall-builders would go hungry."

"Without these fierce wall-builders going out to hunt, there would be no seals to eat." said Apak, putting both arms around Grandmother's small body and squeezing her until she squeaked.

"In that case," said Grandmother, smiling up at Kirima, "your grandson can fill his grandfather's meat cache in the morning. The shaman may not return from his vision quest for many days."

Kirima listened to their banter without his usual smile. *Did no one see Angakok...?*

His musing was interrupted as Grandmother slipped suddenly on a ridge of ice. As she stumbled, Kirima grabbed her.

Why, she weighs no more than a ptarmigan dressed in winter white, Kirima thought, holding her up until she regained her balance. *When did she become so frail?*

When Grandmother had steadied herself, they resumed walking. As they passed the snow house of Yutu's family, Kirima recalled the confrontation in the meeting hall.

"Did anyone's eyes see Yutu in the meeting hall?" the boy asked.

"*Eee-yi*, the mother of Maatu's son has a troubled spirit, that one," Grandmother said, shaking her head. "She has coddled Yutu well past childhood." She nodded toward the snow house that neighbored Yutu's. "Many seasons ago, Yutu bullied the youngest son of Aitii until he cried, and even Maatu took issue with it."

Then she pointed to the two dwellings in the failing light. "But even a woman with dim eyes can see that the families of Aitii and Maatu are friendly once more. The tunnels of their snow houses hold out their hands toward each other again."

The mention of the bully's family eclipsed the mystery of the shaman's eyes in Kirima's mind. "If the spirits allow," Kirima answered in a voice almost inaudible in the wind, "the *iglu* of my grandfather will never face the snow tunnel of Maatu's."

"Maatu has mistreated Yutu since the boy was small, even though the elders disapproved," Grandfather reminded his family. "So are tyrants born and bullies made."

The white mist of Kirima's breath shot out into the frigid air as he snorted. "That is no excuse," he said. "Yutu has bullied me for the last time. He will be my enemy until the sea ice fails to freeze in the winter."

"I know of two other boys who have had difficulties since they were small," Apak said. "Someday my grandson and Yutu may need each other during a hunt, and your dislike may bring them both into the grasp of danger's deadly hands."

Kirima concentrated on the snow, which glowed faintly purple in the fading light. But his normally mischievous eyes still flashed with anger. *I will never hunt with Yutu!*

As Kirima and his family approached home, Gray Dog and the red one leaped up, pulling on their tethers, begging noisily for food. Apak scolded the two, and realizing that no fish was forthcoming, both dogs quieted and dug themselves a new bed in the softened snow. They curled up, backs to each other, noses buried in their tails to keep warm. Kirima sighed, wishing he could see his white dog sleeping next to them, safe and warm as well in his own bed under the insulating white blanket of snow.

Chapter 4

Kirima rolled over on the sleeping platform, drawing the sleeping skins up around his ears. The moss and heather underneath his furs rustled softly. He lay half asleep, enjoying the warmth of his sleeping skins. Then a niggling feeling of unease brought him fully awake.

Ah, yes, now he remembered. The shaman had come! And the shaman had looked at him. Long and hard.

Did Angakok indeed single me out? Why have I been chosen? And chosen to do what?

Kirima sighed. His breath formed a cloud over his head, mingling with the breath of his grandfather, who snored loudly next to him; all family members slept with their heads toward the center of the *iglu*, away from the cold walls. The boy shook his head. *Spending time on such a mystery will not feed my family.*

Without leaving his sleeping skins, Kirima pulled his caribou undergarments from under his head, quickly putting them on over his naked body, fur-side in. He sat up, shivered in the cold, and hastily pulled on his hare skin stockings, jostling his grandfather, who in turn bumped his grandmother slumbering on the far side of the platform.

"*Eee-yi*," Grandmother grumbled. "Your elbow and this old woman's stomach are saying that the time for sleeping has ended."

She rolled over, and without emerging from her warm bearskin cocoon, reached out to lengthen the moss wick in the soapstone lamp. A flame, clear and bright in the gloom, shot up under the lamp. Its flickering light sent the shadow of the drying rack dancing across the ceiling.

At bedtime each night, Grandmother hung a piece of seal blubber on a small bone hook above the lamp. The flame melted the blubber, and its oil dripped down, raising the level of fuel in the bowl of the lamp. As the oil level rose, the wick attached to the bottom of the lamp shortened, the flame danced lower, and the blubber stopped melting. When the fuel level grew too low, the wick emerged from the oil and burned up toward the hook, starting the cycle all over again. In this way, the temperature inside the snow house stayed slightly above freezing during the night, and little effort was needed to tend the flame.

"A clear light and smokeless flame have followed my wife all the days of this family's time together," Apak said sleepily, his head emerging from his sleeping skins as he looked at his wife. "And I see this compliment has turned your cheeks the color of the pink dawn."

"This old man would do a favor by holding his words," Grandmother laughed. "You will make his wife giggle all the way to the slop bucket!"

Kirima laughed aloud as well as he rose to retrieve his outer garments from the drying rack and dressed for the day. His grandmother drew back her own sleeping skins to uncover Kirima's sealskin boots, which he hastily pulled on. The boots squeaked as he strode across the clean snow floor toward the tunnel.

"My grandson is off to the hunt?" Grandmother called out. "This family's meat cache is dangerously low."

"If the spirits are willing," Kirima nodded, "this hunter will meet a seal today." He touched his ptarmigan amulet, proud to be recognized as a hunter in the family. Today Apak would see that Kirima was a man, a hunter who could feed his family and share with his various seal partners.

The boy ducked through the tunnel and crawled outside. The family's dogs dozed behind the windbreak, their backs touching. Although the snow muted Kirima's footfalls, the dogs leaped up and shook the dusting of snow from their coats as the boy approached. Greeting him with a slow *woo-woo*, the dogs pranced, leaving overlapping circles of small footprints in the snow.

"I am hungry, too," Kirima told them, his mouth turning downward to see the empty place next to Red Dog. How he missed the white one! He walked to the meat cache and grabbed a few frozen white fish for the sled dogs and a hunk of seal blubber for his own breakfast, which he tucked into his parka to thaw next to his skin.

The red one ate daintily, holding the raw fish between her forepaws and chewing off the head. The gray dog stood on the fish, tearing at its flesh with his front incisors. He gulped the last bite and minced toward his companion, head outstretched and nose twitching. Red Dog snarled and snapped at the gray one, keeping him at bay. Gray Dog lowered his chest to the snow and raised his hind end into the air, play bowing in apology.

Kirima laughed as he removed the blubber from his parka and began gnawing on it. "Today, I will take you both to hunt the seal," he told the dogs. "Two dogs and two dog noses can warn me about Nanuq. Besides," he went on, "my guardian spirits would be disappointed if others in the village must feed this family forever. It is time for me to give meat to my seal partners and take my place as the head of this family."

This day, I will not choose the easy path. I will make sure I have everything I need before I set the dogs toward the sea. I will not leave in haste. Where are my charms?

The boy checked the inner pocket of his parka. The Chukchi carving of a human figure, given to him in childhood and meant to keep him safe on the ice shelf, was still safely hidden in the pocket. Next he touched the seam of his front pocket, which concealed the small eyetooth of an arctic fox. He grasped the eyetooth firmly. *This will warn the dogs and me if Nanuq comes near.* Then Kirima touched the neck, hood, and remaining pockets of his parka, reassuring himself that he had not lost the various other amulets sewn into his outer garments. All his charms were tucked out of sight; they had power only if they were hidden.

Gray Dog whined, and Red Dog began her low *woo-woo* of anticipation.

"Perhaps I should ask one of the villagers for a bear claw," he told the dogs. "It might soothe the spirit of the white bear and turn its head away from the sealing holes." A frisson of fear prickled the back of his neck, and he swallowed hard. He squinted in the early morning light as he turned to Red Dog. She danced on her tie-out, eager to be off.

"You are never afraid, are you, girl?" He scratched the dog behind her ears. How he could use some of Red Dog's bravery this morning. To venture back onto the ice shelf and into the land of the great bear took all the courage the boy could muster.

Kirima checked the frame of his sled, and, finding it intact, loaded up his *pana, pilaut,* sealing harpoon, game bag, and a large piece of bear fur. He then tucked two sets of sealskin booties for the dogs' feet into the inner pocket of his parka before hunting for the pair of snow goggles he himself had carved several winters ago. Evenings past counting had passed while he carved the goggles from caribou horn, boring the slits for eye openings as well as the holes for attaching sinew ties.

Gray Dog leaped at Kirima's hands, sniffing the goggles with interest. He snorted in disappointment when the boy held the goggles just out of reach.

"When She made Dog," Kirima murmured to the gray husky, "the Great Spirit, Sklumyoa, promised that Dog would never go snow blind. But the Inuit do not have dog eyes. This hunter will need his snow goggles on the next bright day."

As he finished his meager breakfast of seal blubber, Kirima took his time making sure he had packed several small fox skins for warming his feet, as well as his antler breathing-hole probe and his bone seal indicator. Then he rubbed the leftover blubber on his face as insulation from the cold winds that would blow toward him as his dogs ran before the sled. But despite his preparations, he still lingered beside his sled. Nanuq might still be hunting near the sealing grounds.

Finally, realizing that he was procrastinating, he picked up the sled dogs' harnesses. *O Father, turn your eyes away from my trembling. See not my fear.*

Kirima squared his shoulders. "Stand, wolves!" he said, struggling to harness the dogs as they leaped about with excitement.

Red Dog punched the gray one with her muzzle and gave him a hard stare. Gray Dog submitted, lowering his head and leaning against Kirima as the boy fastened the dogs' harnesses.

Kirima checked once again to see that he had everything he needed for the hunt. *The memory of the white bear has not stopped me from taking the time to make ready,* he thought with pride.

He lined out his dogs side by side and attached their harnesses to their tug lines. These lines were in turn fastened to a single gang line that ran between them to the front of the sled.

Then with a guttural bark, the boy jumped on the back of the sled and released his snow hook. His team shot out of camp toward the shore.

Then a voice called out behind him.

"Kirima, Kirima!"

The boy recognized the voice—Baral, his father's best friend. The older man's keen eyesight had not missed the boy's departure.

"Whoa!" Out of respect, Kirima stood on his snow anchor to slow the dogs and wait for Baral to catch up.

Kirima did not wait long; Baral's strong, muscular legs were swift as he jogged alongside his own sled toward the boy. Gray Dog *woo-wooed* to Baral's two dogs in greeting, and only Red Dog's quick leap to the side kept their traces from becoming tangled.

Reaching Kirima, the older man, who stood almost a head shorter than the boy, smiled up at Kirima. Kirima braced himself, for Baral had the annoying habit of ordering him around, not fully recognizing that he spoke now to a man.

"Son of my seal partner, let two hunters travel to the sealing grounds together," Baral suggested, scratching the red one behind her ears. "Two hunters, two seals—many families will be happy tonight."

Following his father's disappearance, Kirima had inherited Baral as his second father and hindquarter partner. When Kirima killed his first seal, Baral assumed a father's duty of praising the hunter at the drum dance in Kirima's honor. And it was to Baral that the hindquarter of the seal's haunch was given. The boy had the utmost respect for this seal partner, but still could not yet bring himself to call Baral *okpat*, "my hindquarter," except during the fellowship sings, where teasing was highly regarded.

Still, Kirima sighed with relief and gestured to Baral. "Bring your sled alongside," he agreed. The boy would no longer be alone on the ice shelf with only two dogs to warn him if Nanuq was near.

Kirima jumped from his own sled as they set off once more, and as the two hunters jogged alongside their sleds to keep warm, the boy addressed Baral. "Has the shaman come back from his spirit dream?"

"This man has heard that Angakok is deep in a vision," Baral answered.

"He will be on his quest for many days. I would like to know how far away from the ice shelf the wooden *umiak* sits. The shaman's helper says it is to the north, many long sleeps by dogsled."

"Pah, what could the helper know?" Kirima said. "Angakok needs him to tend the dogs and repair his sled runners. The shrunken one could not be part of the spirit world."

Immediately recognizing that he had spoken poorly, Kirima's face colored. For although Baral was a formidable hunter with a powerful throwing arm, the older man's other arm was withered from a severe injury in his thirteenth summer.

"You seem to know much about little." Baral chuckled to take the sting from his words. He held out his atrophied hand to accept Kirima's laughter as well. "Perhaps it is time to curb your impatience with others not of your liking."

Kirima blushed and grimaced in response, then managed a forced chuckle. *I have moved away from childhood and I can laugh at my shortcomings. But Baral still speaks to me like a father to a young son, not as one man to another.*

Perspiring from embarrassment, Kirima jumped on the back of the sled runners. The dogs' forward motion would cool him, preventing the perspiration from turning to ice next to his skin. If that happened, Kirima risked freezing to death, and he did not relish the prospect of such a death.

As the two hindquarter partners continued in silence across the frozen land, Kirima continually scanned his surroundings for traces of his white dog. He feared the return of the great bear as well, though he dared not voice his concern to Baral.

The boy grasped the eyetooth sewn into his parka as they neared the hummock ice on the shore. *The spirit of the arctic fox will alert at least one of our dogs long before my eyes can see a bear*, he reassured himself.

"Whoa!" Both hunters cried out to stop the dogs before their sleds began to rebound over the uneven surface near the shore. Baral's snow anchor bit deeply into the ice, bringing his team to a halt.

But Kirima's weight was not enough to secure his anchor into the frozen surface, and the hook skittered across the crust. The sled dogs pulled hard, unwilling to stop by command alone.

"Drive your team to this man's sled," Baral called out. "Your *okpat* will catch Red Dog and help with the snow hook."

Kirima pretended that he did not hear the older man's suggestion. *I will show him how a man stops galloping wolves without help.*

"Halt!" Kirima shouted to his dogs, pivoting the sled back on itself. The lurch of the sled brought his dogs around in a tight circle. He caught Red Dog by her collar as she trotted by. Then Kirima wrestled both dogs to a standstill and finally succeeded in stomping the anchor firmly into the brittle ice.

Perhaps my dogs will cooperate in the company of Baral's team, Kirima thought, panting with the exertion of halting his dogs. Heading out across the sea ice on an uncontrolled ride or expending precious energy breaking up a dog fight would not benefit him. Baral was reliable and strong, good to have nearby in case of danger, and despite the older man's impolitic commands, Kirima was glad to have the older man along.

"*Qetrar,*" said Baral, pointing to the sharp snow crust as he removed his thick outer mittens and reached into his parka. "Bad for dog feet. Does my sealing partner carry protection for his dogs?" The older man took a set of small, sealskin booties from his parka. "I remember in hunts past when my young seal partner left booties behind, so eager was he to find the seal."

"Yes, Baral," answered Kirima with a hint of impatience. He removed his own mittens to retrieve the booties, which were warm and pliable from his body heat. "A dog is only as valuable as his feet. I learned that one when

I was very young! I know how to keep dog feet from being cut on the ice."

Both hunters knelt to check for any ice balls that might have accumulated between the dogs' toes. The cold prevented the hunters from removing their inner fur gloves, so Baral and Kirima chewed the balls of ice from the bottom of each dog's paws. Then, using their own teeth to help secure the laces, they tied the booties around the dogs' paws. Baral moved more slowly, hampered by the disuse of his arm.

Kirima finished the task first, hiding his annoyance when Baral double-checked the boy's knots. The older man also ran his good hand over the ribs and haunches of both Kirima's dogs, then felt down their legs for any sign of injury or ill health.

"These gift dogs are in good condition," Baral said to Kirima. "The son of my partner treats them well."

Baral had given both Red Dog and the gray one to the boy's father when all three of his father's dogs had fallen through the sea ice in an unseasonal thaw. They had vanished, howling, into the black sea along with his sled, and Kirima's father himself had barely escaped with his own life. Baral had then helped the boy and his father build a new sled from caribou hides, whalebone, and caribou antlers. He had delighted in instructing Kirima in the complex task of lashing the frame together with sinew. At that time, Kirima was happy to learn from his father's friend. But he had been much younger then.

"When it is time to stop at a breathing hole, you may want to take the boots off Gray Dog," Baral instructed the boy. "If you do not, the gray one will take them off himself and will eat them in less time than a walrus blinks. Red Dog will not bother with hers; she will wait for something better to chew."

"Yes, the gray one will eat anything in sight," Kirima told his partner, squirming with the effort to remain deferential. "A very young sled driver discovered this for himself long ago, but I thank my partner for reminding me."

Baral nodded, acknowledging the boy's words of respect. "The seals are waiting." He went to the front of his team and gathered up the dogs' traces in his hand. He motioned to Kirima to do the same.

The two *nangminarit* pulled up their anchors and walked their dogs quietly onto the sea ice, searching for the right configuration to hunt the ringed seal. The temperature on the pack ice was warmer than on land, so the light covering of drift snow on the ice sheet would soften the crunch of the hunters' boots, but they also needed to find ice thin enough for the seals to keep their breathing holes open.

"Look!" Kirima pointed eastward, pleased to spot the long, thin break in the pack ice before the older man saw it. "Is that a lead?"

"Ah, these eyes see it, too," Baral answered. "The ice is opening up like a flower on the tundra. Spring returns to the ice shelf."

They turned toward the blackness of the thin channel. The ringed seal preferred to breathe through these small gaps between the ice, thus conserving the energy exerted to keep their breathing holes open with tooth and flipper. The hunters would not need the dogs to sniff out a breathing hole this day.

The seal partners stopped the dogs some distance from the lead. From his sled, Baral took a bone stake, stained brown from its contact with last summer's soil, to which he had attached a long, braided ring. He then used his snow knife to scoop out a slot in the snow.

"You could use this time to watch and learn," he told Kirima. "Let us not make noise stamping snow hooks into the ice."

He placed the bone stake into the slot, leaving the ring riding high above the snowy surface, before scraping some drift snow over the stake. Then, using his foot, he tamped the snow gently down, allowing his body weight to liquefy it. In a few moments, the stake had frozen hard to the ice below.

"This can be done even when there is no snow and the ice is too hard to hold a snow hook," he said. "Yellow water from the hunter's body can make fast the stake, too."

Kirima sighed and nodded as Baral tied his dogs to the ring, the stake a dark brown against the whiteness of the ice.

"Here a red dog and a gray dog will be happy tied next to their friends," Baral further instructed the boy. "It is wise to make fast the tug lines. Any sled dog who escapes will run and run and may not find its way back home."

Kirima obeyed, removing the sealskin booties from his own dogs before tying them to the ring as well. He wished now that he had come out on the ice with only his two dogs as companions. *Will these tiresome lessons never cease?*

Both hunters emptied their sleds and quietly tipped them sideways, making a windbreak for the dogs. Baral's dogs rolled, wiggling and scratching where their harnesses chafed their backs. They sprang up and sniffed noses with Kirima's team. All four dogs waved their tails in the air. Red Dog's tail was the highest, which pleased Kirima. This signified her position of leader among this pack.

When they had sorted out their relationships, each dog found a place in the shelter of the upturned sleds, digging a shallow bed in the thin snow. Gray Dog sprawled on his back, mouth slightly open and feet in the air. Red Dog sniffed her companion's stomach fur, sneezed twice, and lay down on her side facing the sea. Soon she was asleep, feet twitching as she dreamed of racing the wind across the ice.

Moving toward the lead, Kirima walked a short distance from Baral and carved out a snow block with his *pana*. He peeked behind him to see his sealing partner doing the same. As quietly as possible, the boy set the block at the edge of the channel and covered it with the bearskin to shield his body from the cold. From his long, thin game bag, Kirima removed his sealing harpoon and set it in the notch of his harpoon rest. The harpoon rest, which was made from the crotch of a caribou antler, was properly lined with fur to lessen any noise Kirima might make snatching up the spear.

Baral will not find fault with this, at least, Kirima thought.

Then Kirima took out the seal indicator—two thin pieces of antler connected by a cord. He lowered it into the narrow trough of water. When the seal returned to breathe, its nose would lift the indicator, and the hunter would be ready with his harpoon.

I will not be impatient today, Kirima thought. *Yesterday I was too quick to move, and my first seal escaped before I could spear it. Today I will wait for the seal to show me the time to throw my harpoon.*

As Kirima adjusted the bearskin to insulate his bottom from the cold of the ice, he glanced down the lead to see if Baral had settled down on his own ice block yet. He smiled slightly to see that the older man was still setting his harpoon rest on the ice near his chosen breathing hole. Then the boy wrapped his feet in fox furs and settled down to wait.

Chapter 5

Kirima sat by the water until the sun halted its upward arc from the horizon. The seal indicator remained visible in the early spring light, and though the boy kept his eyes fixed on it, he once again pondered the mystery of the shaman's visit. What had he been chosen to do?

I hope Angakok will tell me what I am to do when we return with our seals today. Kirima's heartrate quickened as he contemplated the days ahead. *I know the shaman's spirit quest may take many more days, but must I quell my impatience and prove to Angakok that I am a proper man of the Inuit?*

The isolated sound of water sloshing over the edge of the seal's breathing hole abruptly interrupted his thoughts. The hoarse susurration reminded him of the *huff-huff* of a white bear's breath. Kirima's body temperature rose again, his heart beginning to whisper warnings, as he pictured Nanuq creeping up behind him. The young hunter pulled out the neckline of his parka, releasing some of the fear trapped next to his body.

Pah, he thought in disgust. *Here sits a man as frightened as a ptarmigan caught in a snare.*

Still, Kirima's heart whispered in his ear. *Flee, flee,* it said, *Nanuq is near!*

The boy needed all his self-control not to jump up from his perch. *Listen to your head*, he told himself. *Hold still! No bear is near. LISTEN!*

But despite his determination, Kirima's legs began to twitch. His stomach tightened and the back of his neck tensed. He glanced around repeatedly, sure that inattention would bring the white bear to him.

No bears, he told himself. *No bears on the ice shelf.*

His heart pounded as sweat moistened his inner gloves. His stomach ached, and when one of the dogs gave a strangled bark in its sleep, Kirima startled, his hands leaping toward his face.

Suddenly, the boy's eyes caught the dark shadow of a seal as she rose toward the breathing hole. With great effort, Kirima pulled his mind away from the fear of Nanuq and concentrated on the pulsation of the water above the seal's head. The indicator lifted slightly. At last! Kirima jerked his spear from the harpoon rest, but the seal, ever wary, flipped her body toward the depths, vanishing with astonishing speed. Kirima bit the inside of his mouth in frustration. He had not waited for the seal to take a breath.

My fear made me move too soon!

Kirima settled down for another wait as he glanced over his shoulder at Baral. *I hope my seal partner did not see that or I will hear about it all the way home.*

The sun moved across the sky, lower now, kissing the tops of the clouds hovering above the horizon. Still, Kirima's heart continued to pound. Finally, in an effort to calm himself, Kirima touched the fox tooth hidden in his parka and chanted silently.

There are no bears nearby. No bears on the ice shelf. No bears.

Out of the corner of his eye, Kirima caught a quick movement behind his elbow.

Nanuq!

He jumped up onto the snow block, fumbling for his *pilaut*. *The bear is here! Right behind me!*

Heart racing, Kirima whirled around to see only Baral lifting his harpoon arm high. His legs suddenly weak, the boy staggered slightly and coughed to dispel some of his panic.

With great force, Baral plunged his harpoon into the water. The harpoon head parted from the shaft as the barb dug itself under the seal's skin, toggling itself sideways. Kirima tried to steady himself as Baral struggled to hold the seal by the line attached to the barb. The seal fought mightily until, subdued, it gave itself to the hunter.

Although his hands still trembled from his fright, Kirima hurried to help Baral enlarge the opening of the lead. The boy glanced around as he assisted his partner, trying to calm his breathing as he reassured himself that the hunters were indeed alone. If only his heart would stop pounding! It would not do to show the fear of a boy to a seal partner.

Working together, the hunters dragged the large sea mammal onto the ice shelf as the dogs sent up a howl of excitement.

"*Takiyok!*" Kirima sang out. Despite his weakened knees and shaky breath, he managed to sound glad of Baral's success. "She is very big! She has brought luck with the hunt!"

Baral murmured in ritual modesty, "The spirits of the white dawn smiled upon these worthless hunters today."

The older man scooped up a handful of snow and held it in his mouth to melt. Then, as he began to sing about the seal's courage and strength, he dribbled the water into the mouth of the seal. His song praised the fight she gave him and her graciousness in allowing his harpoon to pierce her body.

He then turned to Kirima, who was attempting to calm his heart by taking long, deep breaths. "Living in the salt ocean, a seal yearns for fresh water and will be grateful for a sweet drink. She will never forget this act of kindness and will repay the hunter many times over. When this seal's soul travels to another seal body, she will give herself again and again to the same hunter who made the gift of such compassion."

Kirima nodded, hoping his flushed face did not betray his emotions. With trembling hands, he held the top of his parka open again, fanning himself cool. Then, turning to quiet the dogs, he grabbed each by the muzzle, shaking them gently.

When the dogs had quieted, standing with sides heaving as they whined in anticipation of a snack of fresh seal meat, Kirima busied himself readying the sleds for their departure. Meanwhile, the older man concentrated on his job of dressing the seal for travel and did not look up as he wielded his *pilaut* with a minimum of wasted strokes.

After lashing the seal to his sled, Baral offered some of the seal's liver to Kirima. Kirima took a bite, suddenly nervous that the scent of seal blood would attract a white bear to the lead. A great bear could sniff out a seal hauled onto the ice more than five horizons away. He glanced around as Baral, singing praises to the sea goddess, bit into the liver. The boy was reassured to see no bear creeping toward the hunters.

"This man is glad to be on the ice with such a worthy hunter," Kirima said, still hiding his disappointment that Baral, and not he, had caught the seal. "There will be meat for all seal partners tonight."

"The sun nestles into her bed in the distant sea. It is time to go," Baral said, looking up to the sky. "Spirit willing, this seal will return again to our waiting spears."

The two hunters repacked their sled bags and set off across the ice. Kirima shot out in front so he could glance back to watch for bears without being obvious. The dogs retraced their tracks homeward in the growing darkness, sniffing for the scent of their footprints on the trail.

"Do you know how to find your way home in the dark if you are ever far away without a homeward trail?" Baral called, pulling his team alongside Kirima's.

"Yes!" Kirima quickly called. Then, hoping to prevent yet another lecture, he continued, "My father taught me to look for the drift lines in the snow. They will tell which way the wind blows and point the way home. If it is dark, a traveler can drag his feet across the lines and feel their direction."

"Yes," Baral said. "The wind always travels the same path during each season and can be a friend as easily as an enemy."

Despite his irritation, Kirima looked over his shoulder. He could not rid his mind of the picture of a great bear following the scent of their seal carcass.

Once off the pack ice, Kirima relaxed. Still, his earlier reaction distressed him. Until the winter of his father's disappearance, the boy had never known fear during the hunt. *What a baby I am,* he thought. *No seal will want to sacrifice itself to continue the life of such a worthless hunter.* When had any grown hunter in the camp ever voiced fear of the land or any of its creatures? And it would not do to ask his grandfather about these unmanly feelings—it was not the way of the Inuit to run to the village elders with every problem. And surely, he would never ask Baral.

Coming into the winter camp, the dogs began to whine and nip at their tug lines. They tried to turn back toward the sea, and Kirima struggled to keep his team running toward the village.

"*Toratsiarpok!*" he ordered. "Go straight! Home is a short distance away. Supper waits! What is wrong with you obstinate wolves?"

Expecting another lecture, Kirima cast a glance at Baral. But the older man, his head tilted to the side, seemed to be listening for something and appeared not to notice the dogs' behavior.

Once again, Kirima had to back his sled to stop his team from returning to the pack ice. He grabbed their collars and dragged the two toward camp.

"*Maiksuk!*" he called to them, "You bad things! See that *iglu*? It is home and a dog's place for fish!"

Red Dog gave an eerie moan, verging on a howl. Gray Dog whined and danced in the snow, pulling Kirima around in circles.

"What is happening?" he asked Baral, tripping over the snarled traces and throwing up his hands in frustration. "They are afraid!"

His expression uneasy, Baral held up his hand, and a frisson of fear rose in Kirima's chest. Kirima untangled himself and turned toward the village.

A strange silence greeted their arrival.

"Where is everyone?" the boy asked again, holding his dogs with effort. "Why is it so quiet?"

"Go tie up the dogs in the tunnel at my snow house," Baral said. "I will look for an answer while you unload the sled."

Made uneasy by Baral's uncharacteristically terse reply, Kirima lugged all four dogs to Baral's *iglu*. The stillness that replaced the usual evening hum of villagers travelling between snow houses to visit with each other unsettled him further. In fact, the village's dogs, usually very vocal at this time of day, were strangely silent. They hid behind their windbreaks and peeked out from the snow house tunnels. No villagers at all were about the camp, either. Were they hiding inside, too? A new knot of fear formed around Kirima's throat.

Kirima chased his own dogs into the tunnel of Baral's snow house and staked Baral's team outside. The dogs went meekly, uncommonly quiet and cooperative. He unloaded the seal and Baral's hunting gear in the dim light of the rising moon. Made thirsty by the work of unhitching four dogs, he ate some snow, then gave each dog a small meal of fish. As he was finishing his tasks, the crunch of his seal partner's boots sounded behind him.

"What is happening?" Kirima asked again.

"The shaman has returned from his vision quest." Baral's eyes were bright with excitement. "You are wanted in the meeting hall."

Chapter 6

As Kirima neared the meeting hall, the small, bent form of the shaman's assistant materialized and beckoned to the boy. He scrutinized Kirima with his single, bloodshot eye; a webbing of thick puckers and grooves, like a wrinkled curtain drawn across the eye itself, covered the other eye socket. Then, nodding to himself, he gestured for Kirima to follow.

The assistant led him to the rear tunnel and lifted the bearskin curtain, his gnarled fingers motioning for the boy to enter. Kirima's heart sped up, and a tide of apprehension welled within him.

Why am I summoned? Could it be...?

Kirima knelt and crawled into the dim interior of the sleeping room, then stood to beat the snow from his parka. Squinting in the light of the soapstone lamps set around the rear wall of the sleeping room, he made out his grandparents waiting among the small group of villagers. Worry lined Grandmother's face, but Apak's face shone with pride.

Alongside his grandparents stood various members of the winter camp, concern etched deeply on their faces. By their sides stood their sons. Most were Kirima's age, some younger and some older. Yutu, however, was nowhere in sight.

Questioning, Kirima looked at each of his friends. They looked back, excitement and anticipation showing on their faces. Two brothers stood with hands entwined, fear clouding their handsome faces. The older of the two, Cikuq, left his brother's side and moved toward Kirima, a frown darkening his face as he tried to catch the boy's eye.

Kirima finished beating the snow from his outer parka, looked up, and moved closer to his friend, standing shoulder to shoulder with the older boy. The shaman's assistant gathered each boy into a small group, then melted away into the deep gloom of the smaller room.

A shadowy figure arose from the back of the sleeping platform. Angakok was there! His shadow flickered and danced on all walls at once in the lamplight, encircling the boys with patterns of light and dark. Kirima shook his head slightly, perplexed. How could a shadow be in all places at the same time?

Tearing his eyes away from the ghostly images, Kirima turned his gaze back to Angakok. The shaman held out his hands, palms facing upward, and gestured to the boys, pointing at each one in turn. The boys stepped forward to face the holy man. Kirima's heart beat loudly in his ears, and he tried to calm his breathing, hoping to appear in control of his emotions.

The shaman gestured again, and one by one, each boy placed his hands, palms down, above the shaman's hands. A faint strumming sensation filled Kirima's body when his turn came. His hands started to burn as he held his hands near Angakok's.

The shaman spoke, his voice resonant in the small room.

"This man's spirit has returned on a moonbeam from its dream quest," he began. "I have learned many things of importance."

The words struck Kirima deep in his chest, and he wondered if indeed the shaman's words came from the man's mouth or somewhere else entirely. The boy's mind seemed no longer confined by his body. He lost all awareness of the other boys standing beside him.

"Deep in a trance, Angakok flew to the horizon. He watched the Kabloonas on the great *umiak*. He saw magic and greed and waste."

Kirima's eyes widened, and his breathing accelerated. He was frozen in place, and at the same time he was aware of a strange sensation, as if his spirit had separated from his body and now hovered over the entire village.

"The men who travel on the *umiak* are not like the People," the shaman continued. "These Kabloonas have skin the color of the clouds on a summer day. Their hair is like the dried beach grass a grandmother gathers to put under her sleeping skins."

Kirima tried to picture this, but his imagination failed. He opened his mouth to speak, but try as he might, he could form no words, make no sound.

"These men have powerful harpoons that sound like the sea ice breaking up in the spring. Their noise echoes across the water as far as the white bear can swim. When they aim these weapons, the holes they leave in the head of the walrus are the size of a ptarmigan egg."

Kirima shivered slightly. He tried to conjure up such a weapon as this, but once again, his imagination failed.

"These men use this sound to enchant their harpoons. They are able to kill from a far distance. They do not need to stand over a seal's breathing hole until their feet freeze inside their boots or row their boats close to the bowhead whale."

How is this possible? Kirima's brow furrowed in consternation. *Who are these people?*

Magically, the shaman seemed to hear his thoughts. "Kabloonas are unlike any men who have put foot on the sea ice. They have driven the bowhead from the Inuit homelands."

Kirima started at these words. His eyebrows shot up in surprise. Once again, he moved his mouth to speak, but his tongue was held fast by an unseen power.

The shaman uttered the dreaded words again. "Kabloonas. They have put our very way of life in danger."

Kirima sent a silent question to the holy man.

How have they done this?

"The Kabloonas have angered the spirits of the animals who give us life," the shaman continued. "These men show no respect when they hunt. They say no words to thank the creatures who sacrifice themselves to the hunter. Nor do these strangers cherish the spirits of those they kill."

Angakok's voice grew louder in the small room, reverberating like an echo around the round chamber. "These men take only the skins and tusks from the walrus. They take only the blubber from the whale. They leave the rest to the fox and the bear."

Kirima trembled. *How can they insult Sedna this way? The goddess at the sea floor will no longer send seals to a hunter's spear.*

"The sea goddess has not yet driven away all the seals," the shaman said, answering Kirima's thoughts. "She still sends the seals, but it is the Kabloonas who jeopardize the life of the Inuit. Their *umiak* blocks the path of the seals that search for light shining through the dark ice. Those seals that choose to sacrifice themselves to the People can no longer find their way to their breathing holes. In their anger, the seals are abandoning the Inuit hunting grounds."

Kirima sent his thoughts to Angakok again. *The People are in danger. If the spirits of the seal are angry, the seals will not visit any of our shores.*

This time the shaman did not answer. Instead, he motioned rapidly, his hands outstretched to the line of village youths. Kirima struggled not to flinch as an electric sensation traveled up his arms and into his chest. The back of his neck began to prickle.

The holy man looked deeply into Kirima's eyes, his gaze traveling directly into the boy's heart.

"The dawn of the Cloud Men is here," he said. "The way of the Inuit will change forever."

Angakok's voice pierced Kirima's chest, penetrating through muscle and bone to rest in the very center of his being. The boy trembled as the words coursed through him, sending a wave of courage and determination throughout his being.

"You have no wives or children to keep you from your journey." The shaman's voice thundered in the sleeping room. "Follow the Fixed Star along the ice shelf north to the land of the summer sea. You will find what you seek where the Earth splits in two and the spring sun rises in the great open sea between two distant lands. Your heart will tell each of you what you need to know."

The shaman took a deep breath. A great wind swept through the sleeping room, lifting the bearskin covering over the entranceway and ruffling the boys' hair. A low moan accompanied the wind, and the shaman spoke in unison with this eerie sound.

"Your time is now. Your spirits are strong. Your dogs are swift. Look deeply into your hearts and listen well. Your hearts will tell you which among you will save the village! YOU WILL BE CHOSEN."

Suddenly the shaman dropped his hands. The spell was broken. A silence broken only by the boys' quickened breaths descended over the group.

Kirima searched the holy man's face. "How will we know if our hearts speak true?" he whispered, unaware that he had spoken with his tongue and not with his thoughts.

The shaman's eyes, black as a moonless night in mid-winter, flickered in the dim light as he gave the boy a long, intense look. Then Angakok turned abruptly and faded into the gloom at the back of the room.

Kirima stood unmoving, eyes wide, as Apak and Grandmother joined him. The boy turned to Apak. "How will I know if it is my head or my heart answering the call?"

His grandfather frowned slightly and answered. "Angakok has told you all you need to know."

Grandmother cast her gaze downward, avoiding Kirima's questioning look.

The shaman's aide beckoned for the boys and their families to follow him once again. Holding open the bearskin covering that separated the sleeping room from the meeting hall, he ushered them into the larger room. Then he quickly dropped the skin, leaving no doubt that they were now on their own. Kirima glanced quickly toward Cikuq, but his friend had turned to follow his parents out of the meeting hall.

Kirima remained in the middle of the room, conjuring up Angakok's words.

"Look inside your heart to see if you are the chosen one," he whispered.

How will I know? If only the shaman would come and give me direction!

But the holy man did not reappear.

He looked right at me. If I am chosen, what am I to do? What can my heart tell me that my mind has not?

Interrupting the boy's thoughts, Apak took Kirima's hand, motioning for them to join the rest of the departing families. Kirima crawled through the meeting hall tunnel and into the frigid night, but once outside, he hesitated. As his grandparents melted away in the darkness, he remained at the entrance, alone, lost in thought, confused, and not a little bit afraid.

What destiny? What journey? What did the shaman mean? Will my heart tell me I am the chosen one?

Then the crack of the ice breaking from the nearby ice shelf thrummed though the air. The sound echoed in Kirima's ears, emptying his mind of all thoughts. In the silence of his mind, his heart spoke clearly. His way was clear.

He squared his shoulders in a shining moment of clarity. A sense of courage reverberated through his chest. Fear and confusion fell from his heart like a great ice wall falling from a glacier. His heart had told him what he already knew.

"There you are, little lemming!" A harsh, nasal voice startled Kirima.

Yutu, hovering just outside the meeting hall, now approached Kirima with eyes blazing in fury. The bully elbowed Kirima in the ribs with some force.

"You think you are as big as the bull caribou and as important as the bowhead whale," Yutu sneered, flinging the spiteful words at the boy. "I heard the villagers as they walked away. They say the shaman said that someone will be chosen to journey to the great *umiak* and save us. But Angakok was wrong if he chose you. You are small and weak and frightened. Just like your father."

Although he recognized the jealousy in Yutu's eyes and the malice in his speech, Kirima resisted the temptation to flaunt his newfound sense of importance. "Angakok said we are to search our hearts to see who will have the courage to journey north. He did no choosing."

Then Kirima brushed past Yutu, giving him a withering look. The bully's face turned red in anger.

Ignoring Yutu's fury, Kirima ran as if on fire into the arctic night.

This hunter feels like a bull walrus cut off from his harem by the great bear. My heart has spoken—these strange Kabloonas must be sent away!

Kirima's running footsteps brought the village dogs to their feet. They whined and danced on their tethers, but no chorus of excited barking and howling followed the boy as he ran. The villagers poked their heads from their *iglus* as he passed, but not one person was brave enough to leave the safety of his snow house. Those still returning to their hearths shrank back as the boy rushed past.

Apak turned at the crunch of his grandson's rapidly approaching footsteps, brow furrowed with concern. "What is it, Kirima? You rush like the river at spring thaw."

"It is I!" Kirima shouted. "My heart has directed me to go on the journey north!"

The older man stepped away from Grandmother to halt the boy. He searched Kirima's face with his wise, all-seeing eyes. With a sad nod, Apak then put his arm around the boy's shoulders, drawing him close.

"I see in your face that indeed your heart has chosen you for the journey." Grandfather's eyes narrowed in concern, sorrow clouding them as he struggled to control his emotions. But his quick glance at Grandmother communicated his thoughts.

Grandmother turned Kirima to face her and took his hand, her trembling fingers holding it to her cheek. "There is much danger in such a quest. Does your heart speak true?"

Kirima nodded, gently pressing her hand to his own face and blinking rapidly.

Grandmother let out a great sigh. "We fear for your life. If you do not return, our hearts will break. If you do not return, Grandfather alone will need to provide for the family."

Kirima had not considered this. He looked down at his grandmother, then transferred his gaze to Apak. Slightly surprised at this new feeling of assurance and resolve, he answered. "For the time I am gone, my sealing partners and their wives will care for my grandparents. I will not be gone long. My destiny lies in the summer sea."

Apak searched Kirima's face again. Then the old man looked down at his wife with a slight nod and a grim smile. A flash of understanding passed between them. Sighing, Apak acquiesced. "Then go, son of my son, and take Red Dog and the gray one with you. They will keep you safe."

Apak released Kirima from his grasp, motioning him to go. Disengaging from his family's embraces, the boy held up his hand in farewell, touching his heart.

Breaking into a run, Kirima returned to his sealing partner's snow house, where Red Dog and the gray one still waited. Baral had staked both dogs outside with his own, and although the two were anxious to escape the eerie quiet of the village, they were subdued and more compliant than usual. The stern look on Kirima's face told them that their time for nonsense was long past, and the boy lined out both dogs with a minimum of noise and confusion. Red Dog took her place in front of the sled, waiting patiently until Kirima clipped her companion to his tug line. Gray Dog did not leap against the snow hook as he usually did.

The boy jumped on the back of the sled, but a voice from the entrance of Baral's snow house stopped him.

"Stop! Where does my seal partner go in such a hurry?" Baral asked.

"The shaman has asked for one of us to go North to save the village from starvation!" Kirima shouted back. "A great journey awaits! My heart has commended me. My time is now!"

"Yes, village talk is as swift as the wind—word of what the shaman said has already reached me," Baral said, approaching Kirima. "But you cannot go alone into the land of the white bear. Wait for me!"

Baral's wife, Oki, emerged from the *iglu* after him, a partially mended caribou skin parka and a bone needle in her hands. "What makes two hunters break the peace of the winter camp?" Oki asked quietly.

"My heart directs me to save the People," said Kirima, holding his dogs by the snow hook, though not venturing from the back of his sled. "Angakok sends me on a journey!"

69

"One boy alone cannot save the People," Baral said, amusement turning up the corners of his mouth. "This is too far a journey for one boy to travel." Baral folded his arms across his chest. "And your grandparents cannot lose another son of their hearth. This man must go with you. I will keep you and your dogs safe."

Kirima's jaw tightened with determination as he looked into Baral's face. "This task is mine alone," he said quietly. "This man will prepare well, forget nothing, and leave impatience behind. And he will come home to his Inuit family here at the winter camp."

Baral shook his head. "No. One boy against the north cannot journey alone."

Oki approached her husband and put one hand on his sleeve as she looked up into his face. A slight smile, visible even in the impending gloom of twilight, lifted the outer corners of her eyes. Glancing at her, Baral started to shrug off her hand, but the sudden hard stare she returned stopped him. She lowered her needlework to her side and drew up to her full height.

Baral took a step backward.

"Hear your wife now," said Oki. "I have watched my husband be a good father to Kirima these last six winters. I have seen the boy grow from a child to a young man. I have watched you, also, but I have not seen you honor the changes in our young hunter."

Puzzlement drew a furrow between Baral's brows. He glanced at Kirima and then frowned down at Oki, who drew herself even further upright. Baral blinked, ready to listen.

"You see Kirima as a boy still," Oki explained, "a young boy needing guidance, a young boy impatient to meet life as a man. You do not understand the fire that burns in Kirima's heart." She reached out to Baral, catching hold of her husband's good hand. "Your strength, my husband, is like the steadiness of the musk ox upon the tundra; it is the power of the walrus upon the ice."

Oki caught the boy's hand as well as she continued. "Kirima's strength comes from the caribou and the wolf, alert and bright, cunning and swift."

Baral slowly turned to Kirima. Oki placed their two hands together, one young and strong, the other, ravished by cold and time. Kirima clasped Baral's hand tightly in his own as Baral returned Kirima's gesture with a firm grip. Here was a son, loved and nurtured from the age of ten.

"How can I let you go alone onto the ice?" Baral dropped Kirima's hand, and turning slightly away, stood sighing deeply.

Once again, Oki took Baral's hand in her own. Her eyes were pleading, but her gaze as steady as the look a caribou mother gives her newborn. "Kirima is a boy no longer. His time is now. He must go alone."

She released him and stepped back.

Baral stood in quiet deliberation for a few moments while Kirima curbed his desire to dance his feet on his sled runners and be gone. Baral finally nodded and held up his hand in the age-old gesture to wait. He turned and entered the tunnel of his snow house, emerging with a bear claw strung on a loop of caribou sinew.

"For the son of my heart," he said, placing the necklace over Kirima's head. "May the spirits keep you safe and the Great One watch over you, just as I will watch over your family while you journey north."

The boy drew his shoulders back and stood tall as Baral hid the charm under the neck of Kirima's parka. Bobbing his head in thanks to Oki, he swallowed the lump that suddenly rose in his throat. Then he lifted the snow hook and was off.

The moonrise cast long his shadow on the snowy ground as Kirima ran his dogs to his grandfather's snow house. There, he made sure his anchor was fast before he began his preparations. He would need sustenance and equipment for the journey.

I will not be hasty, Kirima thought. *I will miss nothing.*

He took a small amount of caribou meat and fish from the meat cache, placing it into the sled and covering it with a thick piece of walrus hide. Then he dug around for a piece of seal fat from the bottom of his grandfather's stores and smeared a bit of the blubber on his face. He tossed the rest of the fat to Red Dog, who gulped it down without chewing.

"This is real. My time is now." Kirima whispered into the ears of his Red Dog. "I am chosen."

The red one lifted her head and *woo-wooed* at his words.

Footsteps approached behind him. Anticipating his grandfather's appearance, Kirima turned, excitement flushing his face. Instead, Yutu stood near the wall of the snow house.

"Where are you going, little infant with the girl name?" Yutu asked. "Are you a coward like your father? Do you flee the shaman in fear and trembling?"

Kirima ignored his rival, turning to the equipment cache instead. *Yutu has bullied me for the last time,* he reminded himself. He dug through the cache and began sorting his supplies in the bright moonlight. Yutu stepped closer, observing Kirima with slitted eyes. "Ah, you run away! Where will this coward flee to?"

Kirima gathered up the supplies he had selected. Then, concentrating on maintaining his composure, he shoved past the larger boy. But distracted by his efforts to stay calm, Kirima did not notice his *pilaut* slip from his overflowing hands and into the snow.

Seeing this, Yutu stepped quickly on the knife, burying the weapon in the snow. Then, when the other boy's back was turned, the bully hastily reached into the cache of sorted supplies and picked up Kirima's short sealing spear.

Gray Dog growled a warning, smelling the anger in the larger boy's spirit. Red Dog put herself between Kirima and Yutu, rumbling low in her throat. Hiding the spear behind his back, Yutu kicked more snow over Kirima's knife and retreated to the other side of the windbreak. He continued to stare while Kirima loaded his sled bag.

Extra sinew line, a flint, tinder, and some driftwood for fuel. Now what else? Kirima kept his head down and looked at his rival out of the corner of his eye. Whaling harpoon! He had almost forgotten the long, sharp spear for hunting the bowhead. *This will be my friend if the white bear and this hunter meet in the far north. A whaling harpoon is long and strong enough to kill a bear.*

Finally, Kirima tossed a cooking skin into the sled after the harpoon, then tucked a large basket of last summer's mud onto the top of the sled basket. He straightened up and hastened to tie his bearskin over the load.

Do I have everything? I hope I have forgotten nothing.

"Make way," Kirima grunted to Yutu, giving the bully barely a glance as he shouldered past him to reach his snow hook.

Yutu shifted his feet, frowning, and stepped in front of the sled.

"Make way, I said." Though he had withstood Yutu's presence during his preparations, all Kirima could think of now was getting away before he let his fists speak. This night of all nights, he did not want to disgrace himself.

"The sled is ready," Kirima told the dogs loudly so Yutu would be sure to hear. "This team has many days' travel before it. I am chosen!"

The boy grabbed the crossbar of the sled and released the snow hook. As the dogs trotted past, Kirima glanced back at Yutu, curling his upper lip like a dog menacing a foe. The other boy stood stiffly, eyes wide with envy as Kirima turned his back to the bully. Then, baring his broken teeth in dislike, Yutu's face blazed suddenly with fury. He withdrew the sealing spear from behind his back, put one foot on the middle of the weapon, and shifted his weight. The short lance broke neatly in half with a loud crack. The dogs' howling drowned out the sound as they leaned against their collars, pulling against the snow hook, eager to run.

"*Go!*" Kirima yelled to his team.

Gray Dog leaped forward, pulling Red Dog off balance. Red Dog snarled at his bad manners, gathered her feet under her, and threw her chest against the traces. Gray Dog, oblivious to his companion's ill temper, galloped across the snow, happy to be running.

Kirima took a deep breath as he drove out of the winter camp. His journey toward the distant sea, the mysterious *umiak*, and the even more intriguing Cloud People had begun. Yet he felt no fear.

"Be not afraid!" Kirima yelled to his dogs, unable to contain himself. "The shaman's spirit will guide me! I am chosen!"

As Kirima sped away, another sled approached, bouncing on the snowy surface grooved by many sled trails. The tall figure on the back of the sled brandished his dog whip, urging his team to intersect Kirima's.

Why, it's Cikuq!

Kirima turned his sled to greet his friend. "Whoa, dogs! Stand still!"

"Kirima!" came the answering cry as Cikuq drew his sled alongside Kirima's own sled. "Where are you going with such haste? You look like the great bear is swiping at your heels!"

"Were you not there in the meeting hall?" Kirima said. "Did you not hear Angakok's words? My heart has directed me to go north. I will save the People!"

"I, too, am on the journey to save the People," Cikuq said. "In the meeting hall, the shaman looked at me. He told me to search my heart."

Kirima looked closely at Cikuq's face, searching for the signs that his friend was joking. When Cikuq did not break into a telltale grin, Kirima paused.

"But the shaman looked only at me! He told me to search my heart."

Cikuq's eyes widened in wonder. "This is a mysterious occurrence! I, too, thought that the shaman looked at me alone, but I when spoke to the other boys, they all said the same thing. Angakok's power is such that each of us thought that the shaman looked only at them."

Determined not to whine like a small child at this blow to his pride, Kirima looked back at the village, which lay huddled white in the early moonlight.

"Are we two alone in answering the call?"

"Yes," Cikuq said. "Their hearts did not whisper in their ears to make the journey. My heart chose me, and I see yours has chosen you too."

Beginning to slump over his sled handle, Kirima tried to hide his emotional struggle. He looked at his friend's sled bag. It was fully loaded, with a bearskin tied over it to secure Cikuq's equipment.

"How can you be sure you were chosen?" he asked plaintively.

"My heart guides me as yours guides you."

Cikuq drew closer to Kirima and leaped from the back of his sled. He set his snow hook and walked to the back of his friend's sled, ruffling the ears of Gray Dog as he passed by. "I see you have packed as much as I. We have supplies. We have good dogs. We are ready. If we are both chosen, so be it. We will go together. Two of us together are stronger than each of us alone."

"This makes sense," Kirima said reluctantly. "The shaman did direct us to save the village."

Cikuq's face broke into a smile. He laid a hand on his friend's shoulder. "Our strengths are great. Our combined skills will aid us in our quest. You are correct; we must keep the village alive. This is the greater purpose."

Kirima pulled at the neck of his parka to dispel the wave of shame that sent a wall of heat through his body. He made a great effort to smile, turning up the corners of his mouth and changing the timbre of his voice to at least sound as mature as Cikuq.

"Yes, the reason for this journey is bigger than each of us," Kirima said, nodding. He drew himself fully upright, hoping that Cikuq would recognize this new hint of maturity. "A community that does not cooperate is a community that will not survive."

Cikuq nodded as well. "Two men, four dogs—we will not be lonely on our journey."

Kirima took a breath, acquiescing. "And we will share the glory when we appease the goddess and bring the seals and bowhead whales back to our shores."

Chapter 7

The moon rose higher in the northern sky as Kirima and Cikuq turned north to the land of the summer sea, the land of the great ocean where the spring sun rises. After their initial burst of speed, the dogs settled into the steady, land-devouring trot for which they were bred. Kirima took the lead, heart hammering with excitement and anticipation of the great journey he and Cikuq had been called to make.

"Now is the time for patience," Kirima said, taking a few calming breaths and tossing the words backward to his friend. "The dogs will pace themselves and let us know when they need to rest. We will need to rest, too."

Hearing no answer, Kirima turned to see that Cikuq had buried himself in the middle of his sled bag and had fallen fast asleep. Kirima's frown emphasized his slight annoyance that Cikuq was already so relaxed at the beginning to their journey.

He trusts his Suka and Akiak more than I do my Red Dog and the gray one. His team will stay near and not go off hunting lemmings like Gray Dog would. But how can he sleep at such a time as this?

To calm his mind, Kirima inventoried the items he had packed in his sled bag. Then, recalling his confrontation with Yutu, the boy tensed. Had the presence of the bully caused him to overlook anything? No, surely not. Still, to reassure himself, Kirima once again went over all his supplies, especially the small amount of food he had packed. The two quest partners were sure to find plenty of game as winter warmed into spring, but were his stores enough?

Finally, satisfied that he had not jeopardized his life in his desire to flee from Yutu, Kirima relaxed against the crossbar of the sled. He fingered the bear claw around his neck.

This powerful spirit will keep me safe from the great bear. I will be brave. I will fulfill my destiny.

Running several sled lengths ahead of Cikuq's team, Gray Dog and the red one broke trail for them all. Soon, Kirima's ears heard only the swish of the sled runners, the panting of the dogs, and the sound of his own breath as it formed white clouds in the arctic air. The boy relaxed, and bending his knees slightly to cushion the bumping of the sled, he drowsed.

The dogs reached the seashore long before dawn. Kirima's sled struck the hummock ice marking the shoreline, and the jolt startled him fully awake. Looking back at Cikuq, he was surprised to find his companion still asleep.

"Whoa!" Kirima called to his team, dragging his foot along the ice to slow the dogs. Gray Dog whined in displeasure, but Red Dog threw herself backwards against the tug line, bringing Gray Dog to a halt.

"Good dog," Kirima called. "I thank the girl who can keep the big gray one in line!"

Gray Dog barked twice in frustration, the sound loud enough to rouse Cikuq from his slumber.

Kirima anchored the sled firmly to the ice and helped his friend stake out his team. Cikuq walked over to the boy's dogs, checking that Kirima's snow anchor was set strongly on the beach ice. To hide his exasperation at being judged, the younger boy gestured toward the sea.

"The wind is building, but at least no bears," Kirima said.

Cikuq nodded. "Yes, the time is for sleeping. Morning will be here all too soon."

"Sleeping is something you do best!" Kirima laughed as he gathered up a handful of fish from his sled bag as a snack for the dogs, who were eating snow to slake their thirst. All four dogs looked up in unison as they smelled the small meal.

Cikuq surveyed the dark sky with its white pinpoints brilliant against the endless black. The handful of stars that sent down a steady beam of light had been placed in the sky to aid the People in their navigations. The many more distant stars twinkled as if to remind the Inuit that their ancestors were looking down though these small holes in the celestial ceiling.

At last finding the constellation that pointed north, Cikuq turned the nose of his sled toward the path they would follow, then motioned for Kirima to come closer.

"Two sleds and two hunters can build a cave to keep warm," Cikuq said, pulling his parka hood over his head. "If I am too cold, I will not be able to return to my dream."

Kirima nodded, a sudden shiver scurrying down his spine as the winter wind nipped at his ears. Both boys turned their sleds on their sides to form a windbreak. Together, Kirima and Cikuq dug a shallow bed in the ice for insulation before unfolding their bearskin rugs. Then they gathered the dogs, two on either side for warmth, and flipped the bottom of their bearskins up over their heads, creating a warm cave for all.

As Cikuq slipped deeper into sleep, his snores intermingled with those of Gray Dog. But a small frisson of fear crept up Kirima's spine at Cikuq's carelessness. If both hunters slept, only the dogs could be relied upon to alert them of the approach of a white bear. He frowned as Cikuq roused briefly to wiggle deeper into the shallow bed, then spent some moments wrapping himself comfortably into his bearskin. Sighing with pleasure, Cikuq slid effortlessly back into the land of dreams.

To hide his anxiety, Kirima followed his friend's example, burrowing deeply into the cocoon of his bearskin blanket. Still, he would keep himself awake by remembering the legend of the Three Stars he saw above him.

Four men were hunting a bear. The bear escaped by climbing into the sky, and the hunters decided to follow it. As they climbed higher and higher, one of the Inuit lost a mitten and decided to return to Earth to retrieve it. The other hunters continued their hunt in the sky, and we still see them today climbing after the bear in single file.

Warm and drowsy, Kirima's eyes closed, and he slipped suddenly into sleep.

Near dawn, he awoke with a start and checked the landscape for signs of danger in the morning twilight. But nothing moved on the frozen sea, and hearing the reassuring snores of the four dogs as well as Cikuq, Kirima lay back in their sled cave as the first streaks of dawn drew veins of dark pink across the spring sky.

When the sun freed herself from the icy grip of the sea, the boys bumped their sleds over the ridges of ice tumbled against the shore and ran out onto the frozen sea. They had entered the land of the white bear. The sleds bumped and scraped over the uneven surface of the ice, their unaccustomed runners protesting with the drag. Kirima halted his sled and motioned for Cikuq to do the same.

"Why stop now?" Cikuq asked. "We are on the sea ice, and travel will be easier."

Kirima scraped his foot across the ice, testing it. "Sharp ice," he called to Cikuq. "We must take care. Time for dog boots!"

Kirima bent to put snow booties on Red Dog's feet, then struggled to secure Gray Dog's booties. The big gray one attempted several times to eat his front booties, but a growl from Kirima and a swift knee in the soft underbelly changed the dog's mind.

"Pah! This gray dog will eat anything resembling food," Kirima cried in frustration, cuffing his dog on the side of his head. "Boots are for wearing, *not* eating!"

"My lead dog, too, wants to eat her booties," Cikuq called out. "Come hold her chest while I tie them around her feet!"

But holding Cikuq's lead dog, Suka, while the older boy tied the sealskin booties onto her flailing paws was just as difficult. Suka was as hungry as Gray Dog, and she bucked and lunged, stretching her neck and trying to snatch the booties from Cikuq's hands. Finally, Kirima picked Suka up and held her above the ground while Cikuq fastened her boots, giving her a smack on her muzzle as she reached again for the front bootie. With a sigh, Suka finally settled down, and the boys were able to line out their teams once again.

"The runners will drag on the ice," Cikuq sighed, pointing to the frozen ground underfoot. "But this man may have brought enough mud for only one journey." Then he shrugged. "Still, the goddess will provide."

Kirima smiled. "Luck and not the goddess follows your fortunes this day. This man brought enough mud for both of us."

And I hope Cikuq brought food enough for himself and his team, Kirima added silently. *I will have to share mine with him if we do not find game in two or three days' time.*

Kirima retrieved his basket of mud from its place near the top of his snow bag. Cikuq, however, was forced to unload the entire contents of his snow bag before finding his own bundle of mud. Kirima hid his pleased smile as he busied himself with his own basket.

We are on this journey together, and Cikuq has had more time on Earth than I, but there are some things I can do better.

"Kirima, you were smart to pack your mud on top," Cikuq said, struggling to find his own mud bundle. "I was not so lucky."

Kirima lowered his eyes with ritual modesty. "My father and grandfather taught me well. But your booties are a work of art."

Now Cikuq looked modestly down. He smiled at his younger running mate, and Kirima's face crinkled into a grin as he felt the initial stage of a strong bond began to form between them.

Kirima took several balls of mud from the basket, thawing them under his parka next to his skin, and Cikuq did the same. Each boy then applied a thick layer of mud to their sled runners and planed them smooth with their *panas*. Now the sleds would glide effortlessly across the ice crust, conserving the dogs' energy and subsequent need for food. Underway again, the boys lined themselves up side by side and set off, but the dogs raced along too energetically; they would tire too quickly if they did not slow to a jog.

"Shhh! Slow down! Shhh!" Kirima called soothingly.

Cikuq's voice joined Kirima's. "Shhh! Whoa!" the older boy cried. "This journey is not yet as old as a newborn caribou!"

The dogs shifted their ears backward, heeding the call and reducing their speed in response. Then they settled into the natural trot of a sled dog: too fast for a man to walk, too slow for a man to jog. Occasionally, Cikuq and Kirima slid off the backs of their sleds to warm themselves. At those times, both automatically lapsed into the customary pattern to stay alongside the sled—two paces walking, one pace running.

Kirima was vigilant, glancing around periodically to catch any sight of the great bear. Although he saw no trace of bears, he could not dispel the lick of fear that raised the hairs on the back of his neck. He hid his feelings from Cikuq as much as he could, but still wondered if the other boy took note each time Kirima turned to gaze in all directions, throwing the hood of his parka well off his head to widen his field of vision.

The days fell into a pattern as the sun rose higher and higher in the sky with each dawn. As they traveled north along the ice shelf, the boys rested their teams for the same amount of time that they ran them. To conserve their food supplies, Kirima and Cikuq encouraged the dogs to sniff out lemmings whenever they rested. As the small rodents scampered through their underground tunnels, the two boys stamped on the burrows where the dogs indicated. Then the dogs dug out the lemmings' small bodies, flinging them in the air and swallowing them whole.

But despite the boys' dwindling food supply, neither Kirima nor Cikuq could overcome the Inuit distaste of lemmings. When Kirima attempted to butcher one of the rodents, his lips had curled in disgust. The People did not eat lemmings. Besides, the dogs needed food. They needed to eat first. The boys' stomachs remained empty; they would wait until the sea goddess sent them something more suitable.

At least once a day, they wet mud with lukewarm water from a cooking skin, or if they had no cooking water to spare, water from their own bodies. This mud they reapplied to the sled runners. Each time they stopped, Kirima and Cikuq used pieces of walrus hide to smooth the liquid as it froze, making the runners as slick as the ice upon which they were gliding.

Although the boys had known each other since childhood, their families had not formed close bonds in the winter camps of their youth. But now, in the intimacy of their cave, Cikuq spoke each night of the girls of the winter camp.

Kirima kept silent as Cikuq listed the virtues of various girls, feeling a slight embarrassment at his companion's avid interest. He then squirmed a bit, recalling his surprising feelings for Liak. He considered telling Cikuq about them, but decided that silence would be a better option until he felt safer unwrapping his most secret emotions. After all, a man did not go through life unburdening himself to just anyone.

"And Yutu's middle sister, Miksa, has such eyes! They draw me in like the caribou is drawn to the autumn rutting grounds!" Cikuq gestured toward his middle. "And my stomach—it aches just thinking of her."

Kirima blushed. *Does Cikuq know that thinking of Liak makes my stomach feel funny, too?*

Cikuq went on, "My mother says it is a sign of growing up, this sudden interest, and that it may happen again and again while I am still a boy. It is called 'puppy love' but is not the love of a man for a wife."

Kirima cast about for the perfect reply, then decided that silence would again serve him well until he felt safer unwrapping his feelings.

"I think you are hungry, my friend," Kirima finally said. "My stomach growls, too, just thinking of food. It has been many sleeps since we or the dogs have had a large meal."

Game was scarce out on the sea ice, and Kirima's stomach growled in unison with the rumble of the shore ice bumping against the beach. His stores were running alarmingly low, and Cikuq's cache of seal meat, blubber, and fish were also dwindling at a disquieting rate. There were no seals to spear, no walrus hauled out on the ice.

Starvation was no stranger to the boys, but now they were alone on the sea ice with no promise of survival. Kirima, and only Kirima, was responsible for feeding his dog team and himself. No seal partners hunted nearby to keep him from going hungry. No villagers with extra stores were close by to help him. He could not burden Cikuq with his need, either. This was not the way of the Inuit man. But the fear of starvation was real.

A few sleeps before, Kirima had spent half the day fashioning two web nets from his extra sinew lines. But the Earth was not yet alive, and the boys found no migrating sea birds to capture in their throwing nets. Kirima was convinced that Sedna remained angered by the Kabloonas' wasteful ways and no longer sent the animal spirits to their nets and spears. Hunger was their constant companion, and for the first time since his journey began, Kirima began to have reservations about the shaman's quest. His doubts overwhelmed him.

Finally, Kirima's desire to hide his fear was overshadowed by his desire to unburden himself.

"Cikuq!" he called to the older boy, who traveled in front of Kirima's team. "Listen. We know that the Kabloonas have angered the goddess. What if she has turned away and will send no meat to our spears?"

Cikuq turned around on the back of his sled and gave Kirima a startled look.

Kirima went on, "What if we cannot find food for ourselves and our dogs? What if Sedna sends us no sea spirits and all we starve? We have traveled too far to return to the winter camp, and our dogs grow weaker each day."

Cikuq stopped his sled, catching Gray Dog's tug line as he and the red one slipped by. Then the older boy turned to Kirima. Cikuq's usually easygoing expression became uncharacteristically stern as his eyes darkened and his mouth drew into a tight line.

"The way of this journey is not supposed to be easy." Cikuq's voice was unusually solemn. "My father told me that many hardships must be overcome before we fulfill the promise of our quest. It is the Inuit way."

Kirima nodded despite the sinking sensation in his abdomen. *What are we to do? My dogs grow leaner every day. My stomach aches and my hands tremble. I can no longer keep warm except at night with the dogs on either side of me. But I am not ready to join the ancestors in the sky.*

Kirima's eyes filled with tears as he allowed waves of self-pity and despair to wash over him. Seeing this, Cikuq politely turned away, and then shrugged, giving a small laugh.

"Whatever fate awaits us, it is not ours to know." Cikuq forced a rueful grin. "We may live, we may die. It is not ours to choose."

One day just after dawn, the boys spotted a mounded shape, light-colored against the stark whiteness of the ice shelf. Could it be a seal or walrus hauled out on the ice? Or, better yet, a baby whale washed ashore and stranded? Stomachs grumbling with the promise of fresh food, both Cikuq and Kirima hastily set their snow hooks before stumbling across the ice, leaving the dogs to fend for themselves.

"It's a walrus!" Kirima shouted with joy. "See what a tall mound the rib cage makes!"

"No," answered Cikuq. "I see a full-grown seal waiting for our spears."

But as they neared the mass, the scent of rotten fish blew toward them, causing their noses to wrinkle in disgust. The decomposing carcass of a baby bowhead whale, blackened and bloated, lay half in and half out of the water. Most of the blubber had been stripped from the body, and the baleen glistened white in its open mouth. What skin remained had been slashed by deep claws and now hung in shreds, nothing more than black tendrils floating lazily in the upswell of the rising tide.

"The bears and foxes have been here," Cikuq said, gagging a little. "I do not think even Gray Dog would eat from this carcass."

Kirima nodded, covering his nose with the sleeve of his parka. "We are many days too late." He glanced around, heart pounding, but saw no trace of bear as far as the horizon. He walked closer to inspect the carcass, noting that all meat had been stripped from the bones, and the bones themselves bore tooth marks both large and small.

Retreating in disappointment and repugnance, the boys trudged back to their sleds, each lost in his own thoughts.

Then Kirima let out a cry of alarm. Seeing the desperation on the boy's face, Cikuq followed his companion's gaze.

Kirima was dumbstruck, but Cikuq let out a wail of pain and anger. "No!" he cried. "No, no, no! Gray Dog, you *beast*!"

Licking his chops and looking mightily pleased with himself, Gray Dog sat in Kirima's sled bag, eyes glinting and tail wagging slowly. The remains of the boy's cache of meat and blubber had vanished.

"And he has been into *my* stores, too!" shouted Cikuq. "He must be punished!"

"That would not bring us back our meat," Kirima said. His shoulders drooped and tears welled up in his dark and troubled eyes. "But this is a disaster."

Kirima hauled Gray Dog out of the sled and staked him next to Red Dog. The female dog promptly began licking her gray companion's cheeks, cleaning his jowls of the traces of meat and blubber that stuck to his thick winter coat.

Cikuq sat down on the back of his sled and put his head in his hands. "We have no meat! The dogs have no fish! We will starve!"

The boys stared at each other before directing their gazes to the far northern horizon.

"I think that now we must decide either to abandon the journey or to continue to fulfill the quest," Cikuq said quietly.

"We have no stores to sustain us, and the goddess has sent no game," Kirima said, kicking at the ice. "We are as good as dead whether we return to the winter camp or continue on our quest. If we continue to the land of the summer sea, we may still save the village, but unless we find food, we will die trying."

Neither boy spoke for a moment.

"If a hunter is starving, his dogs can sustain him for a long time," Cikuq said at last. "We have all heard stories about how our People saved themselves from starvation when traveling far from the camps." Cikuq raised his shoulders toward his ears. "Would these dogs provide enough meat for us to return to the winter camp?"

Kirima sighed deeply and folded his arms across his body as if to contain his anguish. "With no dogs, travel back to the winter camp will be slow. With no dogs, we will have nothing to warm us at night. Without dogs, though, we might have food enough to make it to the land of the summer sea on foot."

Kirima turned away and shook himself violently to dispel the panic threatening to overwhelm him. He gathered Red Dog up in his arms and held her tightly, breathing into the thick fur around her neck, inhaling the smell of her.

Red Dog, the strongest in spirit but weakest in body. Red one, will you be the first one we must sacrifice?

Kirima put one hand on Red Dog's ear, stroking it from the base to the tip. The touch of a dog had always calmed his mind and helped him focus. Now, he needed Red Dog more than ever.

I wish I had never answered the shaman's call. I wish I were back in the village, warm and content, with a full cup of broth in my hands and meat in my belly. I wish I didn't have to decide anything but which trail I should take to the sealing grounds.

He remained a long time in thought, rubbing Red Dog's ear and wiping away the ice that formed on his gaunt cheeks as his tears fell from his eyes and quickly froze.

I wish Father were here.... Kirima abruptly stopped this thought.

His father had been called a coward. His father had lost his life when Nanuq, the one with the damaged ear, had taken advantage of his father's hesitation.

I am not my father. I will not surrender to cowardice.

Kirima released Red Dog and turned to Cikuq. "Not long ago, my white dog, Qannik, sacrificed himself to save me from Nanuq. This was true courage, and his spirit grows strong within me. Are we any less brave? Are we ready to make the same sacrifice to save our people?"

"We may have food enough to continue on and fulfill the quest, but will we live to end our journey back in the winter camp?" Cikuq asked. "The dangers still ahead of us may threaten our very lives."

Kirima frowned and set his lips in a thin, hard line. "When Angakok told of this quest, perhaps he foresaw a bigger sacrifice than just our dogs. Perhaps our destiny is to appease the goddess by sacrificing ourselves so our people can survive."

The pull of responsibility beckoned from deep within his heart as he realized this, and chest expanded as he drew himself up to his full height. He set his shoulders square and approached Cikuq. Putting a hand on his friend's shoulder, Kirima stared deeply into his friend's eyes, looking for confirmation of the choice he knew they had to make.

Clouds of white vapor rising from their mouths and noses, the two boys faced each other for several moments. Though unclouded by conflict, sadness filled Cikuq's eyes; resolve, however, filled the younger boy's gaze. Kirima's sled dogs, sensing the enormity of the moment, lay down with their heads on their forepaws and looked up at him from under their brown eyebrows. Gray Dog whined under his breath. Red Dog was silent. Scenting the stress surrounding them, Suka and Akiak panted, their breath mingling as white clouds in the cold air.

Finally, Kirima spoke. "The shaman told us of the danger to our People. He asked each of the boys in the winter camp to choose. You and I were the only two with the courage to answer the challenge. You and I alone left fear behind and journeyed into the land of the white bear."

Cikuq nodded. "This is true. We journey for the all people in the village. We journey for the Inuit."

Haltingly, Kirima forced out the words he never wanted to say. "It is ours to fulfill the quest. It is ours to be selfless now. It is ours to sacrifice for the good of all."

Kirima looked into the heavens and sighed, squeezing his friend on the shoulder once more. "Are we ready for the first sacrifice?" he asked.

Cikuq gazed at the snow underfoot, his brow wrinkled and the corners of his mouth pulled down. Then, slowly, he raised his eyes to meet Kirima's and nodded. "We are."

Kirima took a shaky breath. Tears sprang unbidden to his eyes, but his voice remained firm, although lacking its usual timbre. "Then, we must sacrifice our dogs. These dogs may provide meat enough for us to continue to the land of the summer sea. These dogs may make it possible to fulfill our destiny. We may not return to the winter village alive, but our spirits will sing out with joy when the curse is lifted."

Again Cikuq nodded, sorrow clouding his eyes. "Which first...?"

Kirima looked at the four dogs. "The one who will give us the most meat. Perhaps Suka? She is well muscled and has not yet lost the coat of fat on her ribs."

"Suka is the leader of my team," Cikuq countered. "She is faster than Akiak and can make the slower one pull when he becomes lazy. Did I not name her 'Fast' for a reason?"

"And Red Dog keeps all the other dogs in line and breaks up fights between the boys." Kirima took a deep breath. "Besides, she is a good mother and passes her talents on to her offspring. She is not to be sacrificed yet."

"Akiak is small," Cikuq said. "He would not provide enough meat for the other dogs and ourselves."

Both boys turned then to Gray Dog, who had jumped up, pushing his nose into Kirima's outstretched hand. He raised his front paws and jumped higher to lick the boy's chin.

"Gray Dog is the biggest of all. I think he is telling me that he will gladly sacrifice himself to save us, his family." Kirima blinked several times. "And the village," he added.

In silence, both boys looked at Gray Dog, Cikuq feeling his ribs and Kirima softly stroking the top of the dog's head.

"When...?" Cikuq asked hesitantly.

"I will take the gray one toward the shore in the morning and sing a song of praise to his fine spirit and his willingness to keep our journey alive," Kirima said. "It will be swift, and he will feel little pain."

Cikuq leaned in to put his head on top of Gray Dog's head. He hugged the dog as the gray one twisted away from Kirima to lick Cikuq's chin. Both boys sighed mightily, rubbing Gray Dog's ears and patting his chest as he lowered himself to the ice, tail wagging.

In silence, both boys busied themselves making camp, the weight of their decision heavy in their hearts. That night, they put Gray Dog between them as they settled down for the night. Neither boy slept well, but Gray Dog slept soundly, lulled by the two sets of hands that caressed him during the long dark.

Chapter 8

Heart heavy, Kirima emerged from their bearskin cave at dawn.

"Shall I go with you?" Cikuq asked. "This may be harder than you imagine."

"I imagined it all night," Kirima answered. Despite the heaviness of his heart, an unfamiliar sensation filled the boy. "I am ready. The gray one is ready. This is mine and mine alone to do."

Kirima took a sinew line from his sled bag and slipped it through Gray Dog's collar. Together, the two of them set off across the ice, heading toward shore. As they walked, Gray Dog began to whine and pull on his lead before turning abruptly to the right. He dragged Kirima around a large ice block, tail wagging and mouth salivating.

A whale! Gray Dog had discovered the body of a beluga whale washed ashore and partially eaten. A large amount of meat remained on the carcass, and even better, much of the blubber also remained intact.

Kirima whooped with joy, and Gray Dog, startled, leaped back from the whale, a hunk of meat hanging from his teeth. The boy hugged his dog, dancing wildly around. Gray Dog joined in the fun, and soon the two were rolling over in the slight snow cover, one laughing and one barking with joy.

"We will need more than my arms and your mouth to carry this meat,"

Kirima laughed to the gray one. He gathered up the tug line and turned, both trotting back to camp.

At the sound of Kirima's hurried footsteps, Cikuq looked up with a grave, expectant expression. But instead of sorrow, the younger boy shouted with flushed cheeks and a wide grin.

"Gray Dog has found a whale!"

Cikuq raised his arms toward the sky in thanks. "Let us hurry!"

As Kirima hitched Gray Dog to his sled, the red one turned on her back feet, eagerly sniffing Gray Dog's mouth. The gray dog teased her, lifting his head high above hers and waving his tail frantically side to side, standing on his toes as if to say, "See what I found!"

As the boys arrived at the carcass, the dogs' barking chased away a white fox crouching a small distance away. The fox usually accompanied the white bear on its hunts; its presence told Kirima that Nanuq had hunted and killed the whale. Cikuq sang a song of thanks to Aukaneck, the god who lives on land and controls the movements of the whales, and to Sedna. But Kirima did not join in. Instead, he glanced around the flat, white expanse of the ice shelf, for the great bear would not travel far from its source of food. Grasping the bear claw around his neck, the younger boy shuddered as he pictured the bear dragging such a great sea creature, longer than both their sleds, from its breathing hole.

Such a bear is powerful indeed, Kirima thought. He continued to scan their surroundings, uneasy and anxious.

Cikuq's song ended, and he foraged in his sled bag, finally finding his all-purpose knife. The meat had just begun to decompose, but the boys were too hungry to care. As Cikuq cut hunks of meat from the whale, he tossed chunks to each of the dogs, who leaped to catch the meat mid-air. With raised hackles and snarling lips, each dog warned the others to stay away from their meal.

Kirima searched his sled bag for his own *pilaut,* but could not find it anywhere. Just as the boy was about to dump the entire contents of his sled bag onto the ice, Cikuq called out from the other side of the whale.

"See how soft is this meat," Cikuq said. "It is perfect for cutting and still good for eating. I can cut it with just my snow knife."

Abandoning his search, Kirima took up his *pana* and found that it was indeed perfect for slicing from the carcass what meat and blubber remained. The liver, however, was missing, so the hunters were relieved of the burden of returning it to the sea as tradition dictated. Instead, the better part of the morning was spent eating and butchering the whale.

The companions found rationing the meat and blubber difficult, but knowing that the dogs were their saviors and needed more nourishment in order to pull their sleds, both Cikuq and Kirima were mindful to eat as little as possible themselves. Instead, they fed most of the meat to their dogs. The remains of the whale managed to sustain them for several more days as they continued their journey north. Again, the boys knew hunger, but not the hunger of desperation.

Along with hunger, the bitter cold stalked the boys as the sun set each evening. Each night, Cikuq and Kirima filled their cooking skins with snow, then slept with the skins under their armpits to melt overnight. If they were not careful to drink enough water, the cold became a more formidable enemy. Without water, the skin on their bellies would not spring back promptly when pinched, indicating a dangerous level of de-hydration. When the boys grew too cold to think clearly, they ended their journey for the day, tucked their dogs around them, and burrowed under their bearskin rugs. Their combined breath warmed the air around them, thawing Kirima's stiff hands and bringing blood back to tingle his toes and fingers.

As the season turned from early to mid-spring, the boys found just enough game to sustain them slightly above the starvation level. But they were careful to share all game generously with the dogs, for only by keeping their teams strong could the quest be kept alive. And though many mornings, Kirima found himself chanting *Cikuq sleeps the sleep of a hibernating bear!* as he shook the older boy from his slumber, their shared difficulties soon brought them as close as brothers.

One evening as Kirima nestled in his sleeping skin, he uncovered his head to look into the night sky, a habit since early childhood. His thoughts went to his father and the mystery of life and death, and stories of his childhood came to visit him over and over.

A streak of light flashed across the northern sky and nudged Kirima's memory about a story his grandmother told him long ago as a star fell and seemed to flash forever. He turned toward Cikuq.

"Do you recall the story the old women in the village tell of the coming of the People?" he asked the older boy.

The silver moonlight showed Cikuq's smile. "Yes. I believe what they said, for old age does not lie. It would pass the time to hear it again."

Reveling in the warmth produced by the combined body heat of the boys and the dogs, Kirima began, echoing the words he had heard so long ago.

"A very long time ago, time out of memory, the earth, hills, and stones all fell down from the sky. That is what made Earth.

"When Earth was made, Men came. They came out from the willow bushes as little children and were all covered in willow leaves. A woman was made, and she found the little children. She sewed clothing for them and brought them home. In this way, Men grew to be many."

Stroking Gray Dog's back and loving the weight of Red Dog's head on his shoulder, Kirima sighed and continued his story. Cikuq reached across Suka's black-furred body to pat the gray one.

"Children began to be born and grew to be men and women. They knew nothing of death and grew to be very old. They grew so old that they became blind. This did not matter, because the land was dark. There was no sun. No day ever dawned. These men and women who lived in the dark did not know how to die, and they grew too many, and the Earth became very crowded."

"I remember the rest of the story," Cikuq said. With a deep voice, he kept the story going.

"And one dark day, there came a great flood from the sea, and many people were drowned. We can still see the marks of the great flood on the high hilltops where mussel shells are found."

Cikuq kicked his feet under the bearskin, mimicking the rise of the flood waters. Kirima laughed, joining in until all four dogs were up and prancing on the boys' legs and bellies.

When all six souls had settled down and were buried under the bearskins again, Cikuq continued. "After the flood, there were fewer People, and two old women began to speak."

The older boy drew a chuckle from his friend as he mimicked the women's voices.

"One woman said, 'It is better to have no day if the People could be without death.' But the other woman, older than the first, said, 'Without death, there would soon be too many again. It would be best to have both light and death.'"

Kirima interrupted him. "I heard that the younger woman said, 'It would be better to have no day if the People could be without death.'"

"Yes," Cikuq said. "That version I have heard, too."

"And when she had spoken," Kirima said, "it was as she had wished. Light came. And so did death."

"Yes," said Cikuq, yawning. "And with death also came the sun, moon, and stars. Imagine how lonely would be the Netsilik without the moon to shine down on us, the sun to warm us, and the stars to guide us at night."

Kirima shivered. "And when the People die today, they go up into the heavens and dance with the stars." He paused, thinking of his father.

Does he, too, dance with the stars?

Kirima pulled his legs up to his body, wrapping his arms around his legs. "I wish for some of the sun's warmth now."

Both boys threw their bearskins over their heads once again to conserve what little heat their bodies generated.

Red Dog burrowed her head under Kirima's arm, and the boy hugged her to him. Was his father looking down upon him at this moment, sending him the courage and faith to fulfill the shaman's orders?

That night, the Northern Lights leaped and swayed against the sky, obscuring the stars and dimming the moon with their brilliance. Sleepless still, Kirima again pulled back his bearskin to look into the heavens. The lights shifted, rising and falling, swaying green and red above him. But tonight, instead of searching for daytime images in the clouds, he searched the shimmering depths for a likeness of his father, dancing in the dark in the next life.

Rather than his father, though, the lights took the shape of Liak, swaying in rhythm to an imagined drum. Kirima pictured her lithe figure moving gracefully as the light from her soapstone lamp cast her shadow upon the snow house wall. He had no name for the new sensations that suddenly beset his heart and body. Perhaps it was as Cikuq's mother had said, just a harbinger of adulthood in a boy's body.

Spring is the time of new life in the land, he thought. *Grandfather says that the birth of a new season will stir men's blood in ways most remarkable. I think it is doing that to me right now.*

He ruffled Red Dog's fur, thinking of her courtship with Qannik's sire one early spring so many years ago. From their courtship had come Kirima's white puppy. This was the way of both men and animals, large or small. Even the blood of the ringed seal and the bowhead whale was stirred, though how such creatures managed their own particular dances in order to continue their life's cycle perplexed Kirima.

Still cradling Red Dog, Kirima burrowed deeper into his bearskin. The faces and figures of girls he had known since birth passed through his mind. For as long as Kirima could remember, he had considered such girls silly children, tied to their hearths with cooking and sewing. But these girls, too, would someday take husbands and begin their own circle of Inuit life.

He, too, might someday become a husband. Kirima began to see them now in a wholly new light as he allowed himself to imagine each girl in turn, busy at his own hearth, sewing his own bird skin undergarments with their nimble fingers and flashing eyes.

His thoughts returned to Liak and the feeling that had overcome him when their hands had touched. He poked Cikuq in the ribs, bringing the older boy upright with a snort.

"Quest companion," he said, nudging Cikuq fully awake while trying to keep his thoughts together and his shyness at bay, "let me tell you about a woman I know named Liak."

In a straightforward manner, Kirima related his sudden and unbidden feelings for Liak. "Every time I think of her," Kirima finished, "My stomach feels like it has dropped to the bottom of the steep riverbank at the summer camp. Is this puppy love?"

He smiled shyly, finally emboldened enough to meet Cikuq's eyes. The older boy ruffled Suka's coat, grinning like Gray Dog when Red Dog flirted with him.

Kirima continued, "Is her spirit reaching out to me? Or is it my imagination?"

Cikuq patted Kirima's back in a reassuring manner. "Be glad for these feelings. It means you are ready to become a man. I remember the first time I felt this way for a girl. It was three winters ago and some silly girl caught my eye. I made myself look foolish following her around the camp and trying to make her notice me at every opportunity."

"What happened?" His companion's boldness astounded Kirima, who could not even meet Liak's eyes without blushing.

"Pah! Nobody bothered to tell me she was married! Her husband caught up with me one day and told me to stay away. I was embarrassed for many sleeps afterward and angry that the entire camp had a good laugh at my expense! I should have kept my feelings to myself."

"Liak is married, too, but even so, nobody has to tell me to hide my feelings. I would be too afraid to displease my seal partner with something like that!"

Cikuq mumbled some unintelligible words, yawned, and turned over, curling into a ball. "I feel a sleep coming on," he murmured.

Kirima smiled. "I am not surprised. This happens quite frequently no matter how interesting the conversation!"

Red Dog, too, shifted position, and Kirima sighed, moving over into Red Dog's warm space. He smiled to hear Cikuq's sudden snores, muffled beneath the older boy's bearskin blanket.

I am relieved that these feelings are normal and pose no danger to myself or Liak. Perhaps I do not mind learning from Cikuq after all, especially about girls!

As if connected to Kirima's daydream, Gray Dog rolled away from the boy and shoved his nose into Red Dog's neck, punching her playfully. Kirima, his reverie broken, reached out in anticipation of a spat, but instead of disciplining Gray Dog for his impertinence, Red Dog opened her mouth wide for Gray Dog to lick. Then she struggled out from beneath the bearskin, play bowed to her grizzled companion, and danced off across the ice.

Gray Dog, too, leaped up, and bowing and prancing in circles, courted Red Dog with a wide grin and waving tail. The two moved off to the end of their tethers, leaving Kirima shivering but fascinated by their dance. When at last the two dogs were joined as one, Kirima gave a huge sigh of longing. As if on cue, the Northern Lights dimmed, leaving only the faintest silhouette of two dogs clasped together in the returning moonlight.

The following morning, Kirima emptied his sled bag in search of food. His supply of seal blubber was depleted; he found only a few frozen fish. He gnawed on these, tossing stray bits to his dogs as he looked toward the sea. The surface of the ice had crackled, and the black lines of open water surrounded each floe. During the night, Kirima had woken to hear the distant cracking of the ice as it struggled to free itself from the shore. The seasons had rumbled beneath him as the thawing ice floes bumped and bounced against each other, grinding their edges to bits. The sea ice had begun its annual flirtation with the spring. Perhaps Sedna would send them a seal crushed against the ice blocks or a few dead fish heaved up on the land during the dark hours.

Kirima was impatient to be off, but Cikuq still remained sound asleep. Hoping to save time, the boy lined out his dogs side by side, but Red Dog had not abandoned her romance with the gray one, and the dogs were as uncooperative as a badly tangled throwing net in birding season. Whining in expectation, Gray Dog jumped the gang line to continue to woo his mate.

"*Eee-yi!*" Kirima groaned, dragging the dogs apart.

He re-hitched the two with Gray Dog in the lead and Red Dog as wheel dog. But the gray one would not remain on task. He turned back toward the red dog, tangling his traces again and pushing Kirima's patience to the limit.

"You wolf, now is not the time to laugh with your bride. Now is the time to pull the sled!" cried the boy in frustration.

"What a noise! Not even a dead man could sleep through all that!" Cikuq startled Kirima as he came up beside the boy. "Send the red one out in front. That will keep Gray Dog pulling on his collar as hard as he can."

Now why did this man not think of such a solution? Slightly annoyed that he still had much to learn from the older boy, Kirima nodded and grabbed Gray Dog.

Cikuq helped his companion hitch Red Dog over one dog length in front. The waving tail and flirtatious eyes of the red one remained tantalizingly out of Gray Dog's reach.

This man is glad after all that Cikuq is with him on this journey, Kirima conceded.

Finally setting off toward the beach, the two boys sped over the land, sleds creaking and runners singing over the crusted snow. But as they approached the beach, Cikuq stopped short, and Kirima called to his own team to halt. He loosened Gray Dog's tug line, relieved to see that his time laughing with the red girl was coming to an end.

The ice was breaking up faster than either boy had anticipated. Huge blocks of sea ice heaved and groaned, rubbing against the shore. Remaining on the back of his sled, Kirima spent a few moments watching the yearly dance of the ice as it rose and fell with the ocean's surge.

"The seals must have left the danger zone by now," the boy said. "And it is too treacherous to search out any fish near the shore."

"Does my friend think so?" With his knife hand, Cikuq pointed across his body. "If we drove the dogs out onto that part of the ice shelf, perhaps they will sniff out some food for us all."

"We can try. But I will listen to my dogs if they refuse to obey, as my father taught me many years ago."

Cikuq nodded. "That is wise." He turned his team toward a more stable part of the shore ice. "Your father did well to teach you such caution."

Still leading Kirima's team, Red Dog put one foot onto the ice shelf, then another. She stopped short and whined. Gray Dog ran up against her rear end and pushed her farther onto the heaving shoreline. Snarling, Red Dog whirled around, snapping at the gray one's face and clacking her teeth. Then she sat, her ears folded back and her nose in the air.

"Hah!" Kirima laughed despite his hunger. "That is what she thinks of our plan and of Gray Dog's rudeness!"

Cikuq chuckled. "My father also taught me as a very young boy to always listen to your lead dog," he said. "And it is very clear that the ice is not safe! Let us see what else these hunters can find to feed themselves and these wise dogs."

Kirima and Cikuq ran their sleds parallel to the sea edge, searching for beached fish along the broken ice shelf. But only shattered, glittering ice blocks littered the beach.

Cikuq waved along the beach, pointing north. "If the fish and seal are gone, perhaps we will find food on the inland tundra, far away from the land of the white bear. We can follow the path of the Morning Star and turn back toward the sea when we have enough meat for travel."

Kirima again experienced a tick of doubt in his chest, but he put it aside, a bit ashamed. They had made the decision. They would save the People or die trying. Still, he was envious of Cikuq's complacent acceptance of their plan.

The boys picked their way through the shore ice, careful to keep their dogs under tight control. At last, an inland path, leading east and free of the sharp ice, opened before them. The boys had traveled only the length of two horizons when Cikuq pointed out a large slope in the distance. Gesturing to Kirima, the older boy turned his sled toward the hill.

Cikuq drove around to the hill's southern side, cautioning his dogs to stay silent. He shaded his eyes with his hands, turning his head this way and that, searching. Following him, Kirima halted his team next to his companion's. The boy stamped his snow hook into the icy surface as he, too, scrutinized the snowy hill.

"There!" Cikuq cried. "See that? A ventilation hole!" He pointed to a dark shape against the white slope. Beneath the hole lay a pile of snow, newly dug, glinting in the bright sunlight.

Kirima's heart raced as he made out the small opening near the top of the slope. Here at last was game! He staked his dogs more firmly into the snowy ground and crept a few paces toward the ventilation hole. He crouched low, making his silhouette as small as possible, trying to move as silently as the beating wings of the owl. Cikuq crawled up next to him, holding his own hand in the air to motion the dog teams to keep quiet.

The older boy squinted into the morning light. "We are off the sea ice, so it cannot be a seal's birthing lair. I wonder if the hole hides something to eat."

Then an oval shape emerged from a hollow beneath the ventilation hole. Kirima sucked in a sudden gust of breath, then gritted his teeth in fear. The contour of the head of a white bear was unmistakable.

"Nanuq!"

Both boys rolled and slid their bodies into a slight depression in the snowy ground, hiding the bulk of their figures from the bear.

Kirima trembled as his heart lurched with fear. But to Kirima's surprise, Cikuq breathed normally, looking calmly at the white bear. Kirima shifted slightly to tuck his hands into the pockets of his parka, lest their trembling give him away.

As they watched, the white bear tested the air with her black nose before digging a larger opening in her den entrance. Her claws were long and ivory-colored, indicating that she was a large bear, fully grown and mature.

Screeee, scrape!

"She does not smell us," Cikuq said. "We are downwind."

The boys watched from their hiding place in the snow as the bear wriggled out into the sunny morning. She pawed at the den entrance and looked back inside. A small white shape climbed into the morning light. This shape was followed by another and then another.

Kirima gasped with a sharp breath. "Three cubs! We must dig the snow hooks out of the ice in case the white bear threatens us!"

But Cikuq leaned toward Kirima, stopping the boy with his calm, steady whisper. "Father says that to be a successful hunter, one must learn all he can about the habits of those he hunts. And to be a successful warrior, he must learn all he can about the nature of those that threaten him." Cikuq laid a reassuring hand on Kirima's shoulder. "Let us see what this bear will do. We are a safe distance away."

More than anything, Kirima wanted to flee the vicinity of the great bear. But Cikuq's relaxed posture showed no overt fear; Kirima forced his own muscles to relax to show his companion that he, too, was unafraid. He knelt, watching intently, and the dogs remained silent, smelling Kirima's fear scent, unsure how to proceed.

Situated at an angle from the two boys, the mother bear turned away from her den and started down the slope. Her time in the snow cave had tinged her fur a mottled yellowish-brown, the shade a stark contrast to both the cubs' pristine baby coats and the bleached-bone color of the snow. The bear cubs lingered at the entrance of their snow cave, digging at the powdery surface of the hill and sniffing the late morning air. One cub thrust its nose into the snow and reared back, sneezing and shaking its head.

The mother bear threw herself onto her stomach, and pushing off with her back legs, slid down the hill. When she reached the bottom, she rolled on her back in the snow, stretching full length and yawning. Then she shook herself and raised her head, calling to her cubs.

Rrrrawr. Rrrrawr.

Cikuq whispered, "Lie down on your belly and cover your hair with the hood of your parka so the bear will not see the black against all the white snow. White bears do this when they hunt seals on the ice shelf."

Kirima looked inquiringly at Cikuq. "They cover their black hair?" he said, eyebrows raised and a glint of mischief in his eyes.

Cikuq muffled his chuckle with his hand. "They cover their black noses!"

How clever of them, Kirima thought. *I wonder how they learned that.*

The cubs paced around the den entrance, bawling and mewling. Finally, the largest cub took a tentative step down the hill, then another and another. With each step, the cub's confidence grew, its pace becoming less hesitant. Then, imitating its mother, it lowered himself onto its belly and pushed off. Faster it went, and faster still. It reached the bottom in a heap, and the mother bear turned over on her back and opened her arms. The cub padded toward her, then latched onto her nipple and began to nurse.

The other cubs hesitated no longer. They began to run down the slope, kicking up white powder as they scampered toward breakfast. The mid-sized cub threw itself onto the snow and slid down the slope backwards, extending its claws to slow its flight. The smallest cub began sliding belly first, but hit a small ridge and flipped over onto its back. It came to a halt at the bottom, staring up at the cloudless expanse of blue before regaining its footing and joining its siblings for their morning meal.

As he watched, Kirima forgot his fear until the whining of his dogs reminded him that here was a fierce creature, well able to defend her cubs against all foes, human and canine.

"We must go now," Cikuq said at last. "Where there are mother bears, there are often father bears, looking for an easy meal of bear cub."

Cikuq's warning jolted Kirima, and the boy's renewed sense of alarm sent his dogs galloping inland. The older boy caught up as Kirima, grasping the handle of his sled as he desperately hung on, raced toward the barren expanse of the arctic tundra. Again and again, Kirima glanced over his shoulder, scanning the horizon behind, until he was sure the threat of Nanuq lay far behind him.

Then he shook his head. *I quake like the ripples sent across a calm sea by the wind.* Thoroughly chagrined, he allowed Cikuq to take the lead, glad that they were traveling swiftly away from the mother bear's den.

As they pulled farther away from the denning site, Kirima's heart began to settle in his chest, and his breathing returned to normal. This release of tension caused his stomach to grumble loudly, and his thoughts again returned to the need to find food for both the dogs and themselves.

As the sun rose to its zenith and then began its slow journey toward the inland horizon, Kirima watched his team for signs that they had located the scent of fur or feather. He was hungry, so hungry.

Gray Dog alerted first. He pulled back on his tug line, swinging Red Dog across his path, tangling their traces.

Cikuq halted his own team as Kirima set his anchor. Despite his hunger, the boy grumbled under his breath as he attempted to untangle the tug lines. Even with Cikuq's aid, it took some time to accomplish this task. Then Kirima motioned to his dogs to stay and carefully scanned the frozen tundra, now mottled spring green, earth brown, and dark orange-red against the white of the winter snow.

"Look over there!" Joy flooded Kirima's chest as he opened his mouth in a wide grin. "The gray one has discovered food!"

"*Ukaliq!* I see it! The nest of an arctic hare!"

Quietly, Kirima drove his dogs a little distance away. Although the *ukaliq* were not afraid of people, the hare would think his dogs were wolves and flee. Arctic hares were so fast that even the fleetest wolf found catching one difficult. Cikuq hung back, his unwavering gaze intent on the hare as he gauged the distance needed to send his spear into the wary animal.

Kirima rummaged through his sled bag for his short sealing spear, but the spear was nowhere to be found. He frowned in consternation, but needing to hurry, he abandoned the search in favor of his long harpoon, which lay near the top of his supplies.

I will use this. If my sealing spear is on the bottom of my sled bag and I make noise emptying the sled, the hare will hear us and run.

He took this whaling harpoon from the sled bag, along with a piece of walrus skin to insulate his body from the partially frozen ground. Then, searching the rocky nesting area for signs of life, Kirima located the scrape marks that indicated the spot where the hare had dug through the snow crust to find willow twigs.

He lay on the walrus hide to wait. Behind him, the dogs yawned and whined despite Cikuq's attempts to quiet them. The boy's stomach cried out, begging for a meal.

Nunam, Earth goddess, I pray you send this hare to my waiting spear.

Kirima stifled a sigh as he waited.

But the goddess was kind this day, and after a time, the hare stood on its hind legs a few dozen paces away, its nose twitching as it cast about for danger. The hare had not yet lost its winter coat, and its whiteness stood in stark contrast to the lichen-covered tundra beneath its body. Excitement coursed through Kirima as he aimed his spear, rapidly cocking his arm. But the hare startled at this movement and leaped sideways on its hind legs, bounding off across the snow. In a flash of white, it disappeared behind a small hill.

Pah! The hare must have heard the dogs whining. It leaped away before I was ready!

A knot of anger swelled upward in his chest, made sharper by the groan of disappointment from Cikuq, who crouched behind him. It was not his fault that he had rejected the Earth goddess's bounty. He had broken no taboos! Had he not prayed that Nunam would send the hare to him? But now she might frown on the rest of his days, withholding her bounty and punishing him for rejecting her offer.

Cikuq called out to him Kirima trudged back to his sled, but he ignored the call, throwing his spear and walrus hide into the bag. There he sat in the snow with his head bowed, pounding his forehead on his knees.

I should be given another chance! Then I would have meat both for my dogs and my cooking skin.

His stomach rumbled in protest; too many days had passed since they had chanced upon the remains of the beluga whale. Why did Numan turn her back on them now, when Sedna clearly favored them by sending the whale?

Kirima's anger stilled. *The whale!*

He had not offered his thanks for the gift. And had Angakok not told the village that the Cloud Men said no words of thanks for the goddess's bounty?

Kirima lifted his head, staring northward across the ice. *Perhaps I am to blame. In my carelessness, I showed disrespect. Now my companion and I may suffer the starving time.*

"What bad luck!" Cikuq joined Kirima, patting him on the shoulder. "You tried. It will be better next time. We will find food."

Kirima looked at his two sled dogs. They had dropped weight, too much weight. He himself felt his own strength ebbing as hunger took its toll on his body.

"If I cannot feed my dogs, they cannot pull the sled," Kirima said. "If they cannot pull, they are a burden, not a help. If they are a burden...."

Gently, Cikuq finished the thought. "This same thought has followed me into sleep, into my dreams these past three sleeps. Perhaps we will have to sacrifice Gray Dog after all."

Kirima could barely bring this thought to the forefront of his mind; it was too heartbreaking, especially since the whale carcass had brought a reprieve. Perspiration rose on Kirima's skin as his empty stomach tumbled. "Tomorrow," he said with an optimism he did not feel, "Tomorrow the Earth goddess will smile and bring us something to eat."

When the day ended, the two traveling companions and their dogs spent another long and hungry night together in the shelter of their sleds. Although Cikuq slept soundly, the gnawing emptiness in Kirima's stomach interrupted his own sleep. His only consolation was a few gulps of water he stored in a seal bladder under the bearskin. Each time he awoke, the ache of his stomach, growling in its need for food, brought a lick of fear. This fear was more immediate than the fear of the white bear; this fear was enough to make his hands sweat and his heart pound.

Kirima took a deep breath as he finally acknowledged the truth of Cikuq's words. They might have to make that painful decision all over again.

Fear and heartbreak kept the boy from falling back to sleep, and finally, Kirima gave up altogether and woke Cikuq at first light.

Quickly, each companion packed a seal bladder with snow before breaking camp and lining out their dogs. Relief filled Kirima when Gray Dog's mating dance was met by curled lips and a snarl as the red one told her mate that her time for laughing was over. The boys released their snow hooks and pointed the sled inland, farther away from the kiss of the rising sun. Cikuq drew alongside Kirima, matching his own speed to his quest partner's.

The feel of the ice under Kirima's sled runners changed as the softening snow clung to the whalebone, making the job of pulling more difficult for the dogs. Finally, the drag became too much, and Kirima halted his sled.

"It is time to make the runners of my sled slick again," he said.

"I am almost out of mud," Cikuq said. "But I feel my sled begin to drag, also."

Kirima reached under his parka for his snow-packed seal bladder. He poured some of the melted snow on his cache of mud, softening it enough to mold, before sharing it with Cikuq. Then he painstakingly built up another layer of mud on the runner bottoms and planed it with his *pana*. His arms ached from scraping the mud smooth, and his breath huffed from the effort. How much more difficult the task had become. How much weaker he felt this day than he had the day before. How much weaker his dogs seemed, also.

At last, both he and Cikuq finished glazing their sled runners and were ready to resume their journey.

"Pull, you wolves!" Kirima cried encouragement to his team. "I have done as much as I can to make your job easier."

The two dogs leaned into their harnesses and jerked their tug lines taut. They set off at a fast trot in the direction Kirima indicated. Before long, the dogs began to whine and prance, breaking out of their trot to pull against the sled in a southerly direction. Hoping that they had picked up the scent of something to eat, Kirima let them lead the way as the sun rose higher in the spring air.

They had not yet traveled far when the companions halted their sleds to check their dogs' feet for ice balls. Kirima's dogs licked his hands, snuffling at his parka pocket in search of seal blubber, when suddenly, all four dogs raised their heads and sniffed the air.

This time, it was Red Dog whose pricked ears and upright tail told the companions that she had caught the scent of prey. Hurriedly resuming their journey, the boys kept the dogs moving in the direction Red Dog indicated, though at a slower pace. Soon, the outlines of many dark shapes were visible near the place where Earth meets sky. Kirima spied strands of light gray hair caught on the leaves of the tongue plant, the arctic willow, which grew only a few fingers high.

Seeing it as well, Cikuq exchanged excited glances with Kirima, and the boys began to follow the path of shed undercoat. Was this the fur of the wolf? Of the arctic fox? Perhaps their presence would lead the hunters to a meal. But first, the dogs needed to be staked out, so they would not run the prey out of reach of the boys' spears.

Remaining silent, each companion secured his team, then double-checked the tug lines. Satisfied that the dogs could not escape to pursue the tantalizing odor that kept their noses twitching, Kirima began to follow the path of shed undercoat, Cikuq close behind.

Walking quickly toward their quarry, Cikuq pointed to the paw marks that crisscrossed their path. They resembled dog paw prints, but were much, much bigger. Wolves! The four sets of tracks headed in the same direction as the boys, following the same scent. As the direction of the breeze changed, so did the boys, mindful of staying downwind of the wolf pack. Kirima's nostrils flared at the pungent scent of wolf, and as he and Cikuq grew closer to their destination, the boy remained ever watchful for the possibility of an ambush by the cunning predators. The wolf was not the enemy of the Inuit, but in lean times, anything could happen as spring turned its face toward the land, blocking the harshness of winter.

Then, as the boys climbed the sloping land, the dark, shaggy bodies of a small herd of musk oxen came into view. The herd milled in a circular formation, their massive heads with their broad-based, curved horns facing outward.

"*Oomingmak*! The bearded ones!" Cikuq whispered to Kirima, eyes wide and flashing. "The *oomingmak* have come to dig out tundra grass!"

"If the wolves take an ox, they may leave us some meat." Kirima's heart leaped with the hope of food. His hands trembled, and he swallowed repeatedly as his mouth prepared itself for a substantial meal.

Quickly, Kirima sang a short prayer of thanks to the spirits of the wolves who had led them here. He ended his song with heartfelt thanks to the spirits of the musk oxen, hoping that his gratitude was sufficient to allow one of these great beasts to sacrifice one of its own to fill his belly.

Then, throwing the hood of his parka off his face, he stopped to watch the confrontation between wolf and musk ox. Bringing one of these great beasts down took many men and many spears, but if the wolves pulled down an ox, he and Cikuq could scavenge the leavings.

The wolves dodged and leaped, searching for a chance to stampede the herd. Short and stocky, the musk oxen were not built for running, but their formidable hooves and sharp, curved horns could defend against even the boldest wolf. The oxen bellowed as they formed an even tighter circle. They stamped their feet and bobbed their heads, horns facing outward against the threat of the lean and hungry wolves, whose dense fur showed dark gray against the brown of the oxen. Several wolves circled the herd, changing their tactics as they searched for an opening between hoof and horn.

"Calves!" Kirima's eyes lit up in anticipation. "The *oomingmak* are hiding calves in the middle of the herd!"

A bull charged out to meet the wolves head-on, snow churning under its large, cloven hooves. As it charged, it slipped on an icy rock peeking through the retreating snow, and before the herd could close ranks, a black wolf squeezed through the slot left by the bull. As the oxen wheeled to reform their defense unit, a panicky calf galloped away from its mother's protection.

The wolf pack was ready.

One wolf leaped at the calf's head, grabbing its nose. At the same time, another wolf ran to the calf's hind end, hamstringing the young animal before the oxen could come to the calf's aid. Bleeding and lame, the calf fell to the ground, and the two wolves were on it, holding it down. The remaining wolves darted toward the herd, snarling and feinting in order to force the oxen away from the bawling calf.

Undone, the oxen panicked, turning tail and fleeing for their lives. The ground shook as the herd broke into a wild gallop, shaggy coats swaying as they ran. The herd galloped across the tundra, kicking up a cloud of snow and thawing soil. One wolf started after them, but turned around to join its pack mates at the kill.

Kirima and Cikuq ducked into a rocky hollow in the tundra, hiding as best they could. If the wolves caught sight of the hunters, then the pack, aroused by the act of killing, could turn on the boys as easily as they had brought down the calf.

Sounds of gnashing teeth and snarling voices filled the air, telling the boys that the wolves had ripped open the hide of the calf and had begun to feed. The calf let out a last strangled cry, and all was silent but for the crunch of bone and the tearing of flesh.

The boys lay in the dim hollow until all was quiet. Peering over the lip of the depression, Kirima saw the wolf pack leaving the calf carcass and loping across the tundra in an easterly direction, following the scent of the stampeding musk oxen.

"Stay here, Cikuq! I will bring my sled and our knives so we can cut up what is left of the calf!"

Hurrying back to his sled, Kirima quickly found Cikuq's *pilaut* and began to search his sled bag for his own all-purpose knife. The *pana*, his snow knife, would not be adequate; the *pilaut* was the proper one to flense the carcass and salvage what meat and fat he could.

My pilaut*!* Kirima upended his sled bag in alarm. *Where is it?*

Alarmed, Kirima widened the opening in the top of his sled bag. His agitation grew as he pawed through the jumbled contents. *I could not have forgotten my most important knife! I packed with care, though Yutu tried to distract me....*

The boy sat back on his heels. Yutu! The bully had stolen Kirima's *pilaut*!

But there was no time to dwell on the bully, for Cikuq was gesturing wildly for Kirima to hurry. Although the wolves had galloped away in pursuit of the fleeing herd, there was always the danger that they could return to the calf.

With a yip, Kirima leaped on his sled and directed his dogs to the mutilated carcass. The wolf pack had not devoured the entire calf; still, not much of it remained. Its hide was slashed beyond all practical use, but even so, the boys would not waste a scrap.

Kirima handed Cikuq his knife. "This hunter is glad to see you have your *pilaut* for this task. Mine is missing. I will do what I can with my *pana*."

"It is most likely lying at the bottom of your sled bag," Cikuq said. "You can use your snow knife to scrape off the fat from the skin after I loosen it from the carcass."

Kirima peered over his companion's shoulder as Cikuq began to cut away the hide and what little meat remained on the calf. Kirima joined him, scraping and flensing the fat away.

"The calf has already begun to grow an undercoat." Cikuq ran his hand against the hair of the calf. "I will take half to bring back to my mother. My family's clothing has grown thin—this calf's *qiviut* is not much, but it will help provide new insulation for our parkas."

Kirima smiled. "My grandmother uses *qiviut* also in our clothing. I had forgotten this."

"Here, take the rest." Cikuq held out some of the calf's soft undercoat. "We are now *oomingmak* partners and share equally."

After salvaging as much as they could, the boys bundled the meat in the scraps of hide. Then, carefully dividing the calf into equal portions, the boys fed their dogs. Red Dog was characteristically polite in accepting the handful, but Gray Dog, Suka, and Akiak leaped wildly toward the offerings, snarling at each other in their eagerness to defend their share.

"Back, dogs!" Cikuq yelled.

"Stop!" Kirima shouted.

After much scuffling and a few well-aimed kicks by both boys, the dogs were separated and fed. Then the two companions turned to the remains of the carcass.

"The younger the *oomingmak,* the better the flavor," Cikuq mumbled as he bolted his portion with swift bites.

Kirima ate more slowly, savoring every bite, feeling the warmth of the meal flow from his belly to his arms and legs.

"The flavor comes from the fat," Kirima said, taking a few small bites of musk ox fat. "And the *oomingmak* has fat running through the inside of the meat, too. Not even caribou have this."

Despite the meal, though, Kirima was still angry that Yutu had put his life in jeopardy. The boy picked up his *pana*, putting it on top of the meat bundle. He was unhappy that he had not been able to assist in the butchering of the calf remains, meager as they were. Using his snow knife to cut up the calf would have been hazardous. He could have cut his hand in the process, a cut which might fester in the absence of soothing summer herbs and oils. He snorted in disgust. Yutu was to blame!

"My skinning knife was not in my sled," he said, opening up the topic that had weighed on his mind throughout the butchering and eating of the calf. "I think Yutu stole my *pilaut* back in the winter camp."

"Pah, Yutu! My mother says Yutu has been touched by Keelut, the evil spirit that often comes to Earth as a dog."

Kirima nodded, gratified that his friend saw the bully in the same way. "That dog must have been present when Yutu was born. He has been cruel all his life. And this man has had to protect the younger boys in the village from his vicious ways."

"Last summer, Yutu punctured holes in my *kayak* right before the fishing season," Cikuq said. "I saw him do it. But nothing of consequence happened to him to make him think about what an evil deed that was."

"That was indeed evil. Long ago, he kicked the head of my white puppy for no reason except to be cruel. My grandfather says Yutu was mistreated as a child, so he became a bully. But my family also believes Yutu spent too much time in his mother's hood and thinks he can do as he pleases no matter what the consequences." Kirima frowned with displeasure. "I hope his family does not join ours on the trail of the caribou when this season turns to summer."

"That is not good to imagine," Cikuq said with a consoling pat on his companion's shoulder. "He would be a burden, not a helpmate, for any of you."

Kirima took many deep breaths to dispel his emotions. He wanted his anger to dissolve like the sweet river water that flows into the ocean and is lost.

"I am happy beyond measure that I did not embark on this journey alone," Kirima said. "If Yutu indeed took my *pilaut*, my life would have been in jeopardy. That bully's actions would have endangered all the People, not just this man."

"Yes," Cikuq said. "And this quest is bigger than either of us."

A wave of heat engulfed Kirima at Cikuq's words. He pulled the neck of his parka out, releasing some of the warm air next to his body. "Yes, blaming Yutu will not help us on our journey. Now is the time to set this aside." He took another bite of calf meat. "We must honor our people by speaking kindly and not in anger. It is the Inuit way."

Cikuq swallowed and smiled. "I understand what you say. It is the way of a man." Standing, Cikuq licked the last of the calf fat from his lips. "Yutu is of no consequence out here on the tundra. We need to find more food." Cikuq patted Kirima again. "Let us go."

Still savoring the taste of *oomingmak*, the boys carefully packed their bundles of meat in their sled bags, deep enough so the dogs would not worry the sled bags, yet high enough so the boys could grab a quick snack for the dogs if they began to tire.

With great effort, Kirima turned his mind away from thoughts of Yutu and took another deep breath. The scent of the tundra had changed, and the air held more than just the promise of spring. The boy smelled the thick scent of mud, earthy and rich, while the greening of the tundra brought him the faint scent of shoot and stem. The air itself carried the hint of willow and sedge.

Slowly, Kirima rearranged some of the gear in his sled bag. "I can scent the arrival of spring in the air. The season is finally turning. There will be seals and shore birds for us to hunt if we turn back toward the sea."

"Yes," Cikuq agreed. "The time has come to continue our journey into the land of the white bear."

Kirima shuddered slightly, but said nothing. His hand went involuntarily to the bear claw amulet around his neck, but the prospect of food outweighed any other consideration.

By mid-morning, the sun had poked her face though the white puffs of the early morning clouds and sent her warming rays across the land. Kirima opened the neck of his parka to cool himself, then finally removed it completely, relishing the feeling of lightness on his shoulders and stretching to feel the full flexibility of his arms. Red Dog's thick winter coat was beginning to thin, sending tufts of buff-colored undercoat poking through the russet guard hairs on her haunches.

When the boys again stopped to rest the dogs, Kirima climbed a small rise and looked across the flat landscape. The retreating snow left behind patches of brown as mud and thawed soil reclaimed the land. Mosses and lichens added their green and orange color to the tundra floor, and grasses, long buried through the winter, poked their heads from the whiteness of the snow. In some places, the dried grasses from last summer's growing season lay in tangled clumps, dark against the backdrop of what little snow remained. Kirima noted the saxifrage shooting up from the thin soil. Soon the little plant would flower, hiding its petals close to the ground to protect them from the ever-present arctic wind. Kirima licked his chapped lips, remembering the sweet and tangy taste of the purple saxifrage blossoms, which supplied vital nutrients to the People and which accompanied the beginning of the musk ox calving season.

"Look," Kirima said, pointing toward a stand of tall grass with white heads seeming almost to explode on their short stalks. "*Qitsualik!* We can collect the flower puffs to use as wicks in our lamps!"

Awa-awra. Awa-awra.

The faint cry floated in the dry air just as Kirima turned back to Cikuq. He recognized the sound immediately.

Kirima's voice rang out across the thawing land. "Listen! Something to eat!" He scrambled down the hill and found Cikuq asleep beside his sled.

"Wake up! The time for hunting is here! Oldsquaw!"

Cikuq stretched, yawning, and blinked at his companion before pulling himself upright on the sturdy rail side of his sled. "Ducks?"

"Ducks!" Excitement built in Kirima's chest. "They are migrating toward the open water. But we must wait for nightfall. Do you know how to hunt them?"

Relief rushed over Kirima as Cikuq nodded.

"They will be difficult to bring down if they see us," Cikuq explained. "That is why night is the best time to hunt. First, we must prepare. Let us search for a circle of stones."

Kirima located the special soil formation first. The repeated thawing and freezing of the land caused the rock particles in the soil to separate into neat circles, with the larger stones circling the outside and the finer gravel and bits of sand on the inside. From these circles, Cikuq chose several round, matched stones, each twice the size of a ptarmigan egg, and spent the rest of the afternoon showing Kirima how to fashion a bola from the stones, some bits of sinew, and the remnants of his throwing net. He took his time weaving a small mesh cup around each of the stones, then attaching them to longer sinew thongs.

Kirima took much longer to fashion his own bola, but finally, just before nightfall dimmed his sight and hunger made his hands tremble, he wove the thongs to a bit of the salvaged tail from the musk ox calf, forming a handle. At last, he had a throwing weapon.

The dogs alerted to the next flock of ducks flying toward them. They watched with pricked ears and slightly waving tails as the longtails swooped and dove, constantly changing their flight pattern.

When the clouds had joined the sun on the other side of the sea, the companions motioned to the dogs to be silent, then stepped quietly away from camp, following the sound of the ducks. To keep the bola's strings from tangling, Cikuq wrapped them around his forehead, and Kirima followed his example. The stone weights hung down over each boy's neck and bumped along as the hunters walked toward the patches of last summer's puff grass, now glistening with frost in the rising moonlight. Finding cover behind the tallest stand of *oitsualik*, the two sat down to wait.

There is still much I can learn from Cikuq. Kirima looked sideways at his friend's profile and touched his own bola. *This man is grateful for his companionship.*

Awa-awra. Awa-awra.

Again, the harsh sound of the longtail duck broke the silence.

"Do you know what to do?" Cikuq whispered.

Kirima drew his feet under him and crouched low, readying the bola. "I have seen it done, but I will wait for you to do it first." Kirima paused, a smile on his face and a mischievous glint in his eye. "Unless, of course, you intend to sleep through their migration."

Cikuq's answering smile turned to excitement as they heard the ducks approach.

Awa-awra. Awa-awra.

There! Flying toward them was the flock of oldsquaw on their way from the open ocean to the deep, inland lakes. Their white underbellies stood out in stark relief against the night sky, and the rasp of their nasal calls disrupted the arctic calm. Several of the ducks extended their feet, glistening in the moonlight, as they prepared to land near the edge of the boys' grass blind.

When the birds overhead were as close to the boys as the length of two sleds, Cikuq sprang up and twirled the bola over his head. Almost simultaneously, he took aim and threw with a coordinated motion of his foot, legs, shoulders, and arms. Kirima blinked at the sudden *zoot!* of the bola as it flew, spinning through the air in its trajectory toward the front of the lead duck's flight path. The bola struck the bird, the sinews wrapping themselves around the oldsquaw's legs. The duck struggled to stay aloft, wings flapping wildly, but the weight of the bola brought the bird to the ground. The rest of the flock barked in alarm, reforming as they wheeled away into the moonlight.

The older boy sprinted to the fallen duck, pinning it with his foot and yanking its head forcefully over its back. With a crack, the duck's neck broke, and, grinning, Cikuq held up the limp makings of a meal. Pausing to sing a quick song of thanks to the spirit of the duck, Cikuq stroked the long, black tail feathers; its winter plumage had already begun molting as it changed into its summer clothing.

Kirima waited for the flight of ducks to turn back toward their nesting grounds. When the flock was nearly upon him, he leaped up and threw his bola, launching it with all his might. It arced through the air before sailing several arm lengths away from the feet of the nearest duck. The hiss of the bola sent the ducks wheeling again in a large, panicked circle.

"Pah!" Cikuq said. "Too bad. Here they come once more. Try it again." He hefted his own bola, searching the sky for the sight of white belly feathers.

Kirima missed his duck a second time, but Cikuq's bola hit its mark, bringing down another oldsquaw with a rattle of stones and a loud squawk.

"Food! We have food! Enough for all of us tonight. And more on the wing!" Kirima's joy over their success contained no hint of envy. "How many more can you bring down?"

The boys shifted position, leaving the blind and walking quietly to a new intercept behind another tall clump of puff grass. Though Kirima's aim improved, the three additional ducks that fell were by Cikuq's bola.

I will practice this art when we return home until I can hit a target as easily as Cikuq. Kirima smiled at his companion. *And I will not sleep until I do!*

"We must thank to the spirits who sent these ducks to us," Cikuq said. "And thank the spirits who guided our sleds to their migration route."

"And thank the Earth goddess for sending us this food and sparing our dogs," Kirima replied with a choke in his voice. He was anxious to return to their camp and rub the ears of his two faithful sled dogs.

Chapter 9

At sundown each day, the boys hitched their dogs to their sleds and dutifully followed the path of the stars leading them north. Night after night they traveled, but despite his faith in Angakok's words, Kirima began to despair of ever reaching the land that kissed the summer sea.

"Cikuq, we have followed the spring stars, just as Angakok instructed," Kirima called out at last, slowing his dogs so his friend could swing alongside. "But perhaps we are not following the correct path." He frowned. "If only Angakok had told us how many days the journey would last!"

Cikuq's shrug was visible even in the darkness. "He said it would take as long as it would take. Did he not come from that land in his dream quest?"

Kirima looked sideways at his friend, brow wrinkling in surprise. "The shaman told you that? He did not mention anything to me." The boy could not hide the disappointment in his voice, and he cleared his throat to dispel the touch of jealousy that pricked his heart like e mentioa broken fish hook.

"Perhaps you left the village in too much haste," Cikuq said, a lilt in his voice. "I set off running my dogs at full speed before I saw you ahead of me!"

Kirima asked no more questions. *I am certain I packed with care. And I wonder how and when the shaman imparted this knowledge to Cikuq.*

Then he bit his lip. *No. Instead of jealousy, I will be grateful for Cikuq's knowledge.*

Kirima's heart swelled with pride at this thought, but he quickly tamped down that emotion. Pride had no place in the life of an Inuit man.

Just before dawn, Kirima noticed that his sled runners glided differently across the surface beneath him. The rocky sand beneath the covering of snow added additional drag to his sled, and all four dogs panted with the extra exertion. Then, through the gloom that still hovered over the land, Kirima made out a great split in the sea ice and a black expanse of ocean before him. The grinding groan of thawing ice blocks bumping against the distant shore was music to his ears.

Was this the land of the summer sea at last?

Kirima called out to Cikuq. "Look!" He pointed as he echoed the shaman's words. "We will find what we seek where the earth splits in two and the spring sun rises in the great open sea between two distant lands— have we found our way at last?"

"Perhaps. But it is almost dawn," Cikuq said, his voice calm, his excitement muted. "We will need its light to see if we have reached our destination."

The companions halted their sleds and busied themselves snacking the dogs and awaiting the sunrise. As Kirima settled into his sled, Cikuq set his snow hook and sat down atop his own sled bag, folding his arms across his body. He slumped lower and lower until he lay comfortably supine. A slight snore escaped his lips, and Kirima, drifting into sleep himself, smiled at the sound.

When Kirima woke with a start some time later, the sun already shone brightly in the sky. The boy rose at once, shielding his eyes against the glare as he searched the landscape. Then he tugged Cikuq's arm, waking the older boy, who blinked against the bright glow of sunshine that assaulted his eyes.

Although his heart beat with excitement, Kirima steadied his arm as he pointed. His earlier doubt spilled from his heart like the summer river tumbling toward the sea. "There is the land that splits in two! Here is the ocean lying between. And the spring sun is rising out of the sea!"

"We found it!" Cikuq's own cry of joy echoed in the early morning sunlight.

Wasting no time, the two voyagers readied their sleds and ventured out on the still-frozen sea ice, keeping parallel to the shore. There, in the distance, loomed a strange silhouette, dark against the lighter backdrop of the horizon. The sea mist hovering at the horizon blew its way shoreward, obscuring the shape in front of them.

Despite his excitement, Kirima's heart leaped in fear. *Nanuq? Is it Nanuq?*

But no.

As the companions drew closer, the shape grew in size, carving an unfamiliar silhouette into the sky. Two long arms and one shorter one, all just visible through the fog, reached up from the body of the thing, seeming to touch the very heavens. What could it be?

Kirima slowed his sled. "Is this it?" he called back to Cikuq. "Is this the great *umiak*?" His heartbeat accelerated once again at the prospect.

Cikuq drew alongside him and frowned. "If this is the great *umiak*, it would be wise to keep our distance and wait to approach until we can see what danger there may be. The sea mists are too thick to make out what is before us."

"Yes," Kirima conceded. "And the evil sea spirits that sent the great *kayak* here might make mischief if we come too near."

The boys retreated from the shoreline, stamping their feet on their sled platforms as they did to keep their feet from turning numb. A frigid wind kicked up, and Kirima shivered.

The companions waited on the beach as the day progressed. The cold intensified as a sudden, rigid snap halted the spring thaw, thickening the shore ice. Tiny crystals of ice fog clung to the boys' parkas, their sleds, and the dogs' coats, giving them an otherworldly, ghost-like look.

The dogs were uncharacteristically restless, howling into the wind and pulling against the traces snugged to their collars. Then Gray Dog and Suka began snarling at each other, snapping their teeth. Red Dog leaped to the gray one's aid, but before the fight could escalate, the boys pulled the dogs apart.

Finally, Cikuq spoke up. "We do not yet know if our travels have brought us to the end of our journey or just to the beginning of a new quest," he said. "We must wait until we are sure. Let us move landward, far away from the *umiak*, and make camp. There we will wait in comfort for a sign to show us how to proceed."

"Yes," Kirima said. "This plan is sound. We must be patient. In the meantime, our sleds cry out for attention."

The boys moved inland and made camp, spending the rest of the day tightening up the frames of their sleds, which had suffered greatly during their journey. Busy as they were, they took many breaks to peer through the heavy fog shrouding the land. But no sign was forthcoming.

The older boy sighed as he helped Kirima re-stitch his sled covering to its frame. "If we do not receive a sign today," he said, "let us travel back to the *umiak* in the morning. Perhaps the fog will have lifted, and we can see what we might see."

The day dragged on, but finally, the sun lowered herself into the sea, a white orb glimmering through the veil of sea mist. Anticipation of the dangers the white dawn might bring made for fitful sleep. The wind moaned and sighed, as if the evil spirits of the sea intoned their ominous chanting. As Kirima dug himself deeper into his sleeping skins, he pulled Red

Dog to his side and wrapped his arms around her comforting warmth. Red Dog hummed a throaty purr of contentment, then followed it with a small whimper.

If only I had Cikuq's ability to fall instantly asleep and remain so for the entire night!

Was not the older boy bothered by fearful and unsettling thoughts? Or had he learned to overcome them, as a man of the People must? Kirima's dreams, when he finally fell asleep, were full of images of shaman masks, white bears, and the endless, barren tundra.

The early morning mists still covered the land, but the ice fog had disappeared, and the dawn revealed the thick layer of frost that had re-formed on the sled runners. Kirima groaned, kicking at the ice in frustration. Their journey could not be resumed until the boys had released the runners from the ice.

As they struggled to free the sleds, Cikuq kept up a steady stream of talk, and although Kirima attempted to join in, he could not help casting glances back over his shoulder. His dreams had renewed his fears of Nanuq, and through the morning fog, Kirima strained to see whether a white bear might be creeping in ambush.

Gradually, though, the fog began to clear. Kirima abandoned his efforts to free his sled and turned to squint toward the sea. He peered across the foggy land, impatience hammering at his heart as he tried to identify the indistinct outline in the haze. If the shape were indeed that of an *umiak*, it was like no *kayak* Kirima had ever imagined.

A sudden lift of the sea mist brought the answer. Kirima's heart contracted, for although the great silhouette still tilted unmoving in the distance, a second large and unfamiliar shape had now joined the first at the horizon.

Kirima glanced back at the dogs, but they still lay dozing nearby; they did not alert to a bear. What could it be?

The Raven. It is the Raven playing tricks on me. The old women say that Raven became bored after creating Earth, so he often fools the People to amuse himself. Raven made another shape near the first one and is trying to convince me it is a white bear.

"Kirima, are you daydreaming?" Cikuq called suddenly.

The younger boy shook himself, attempting to return Cikuq's grin as he returned to his task.

I have no reason to fear, Kirima reassured himself. *My dog's noses tell me the truth. No bears today.* He kicked the ice off the back of the sled platform, sending a chunk flying.

After freeing the sleds at last, the companions smoothed the bottoms of their runners, then set off, the sleds running toward the sea with barely a whisper as the dogs ran swiftly over the surface crust. Only the sound of the dogs' huffing broke the silence of the morning.

As Kirima and Cikuq drew close to the edge of sea, Kirima drew a sharp breath of recognition.

"Look, Cikuq! It is as the shaman described!" Kirima screwed up his face with the effort to remember Angakok's words. "Larger the drum dance hall, larger than our entire winter village. Many antlers from giant caribou, hung with white skins, many people high."

"Whoa!" cried Cikuq, slowing his dogs to a walk. Mouth open and eyes wide, he glanced at his traveling companion, utter astonishment showing on his wind-burned face.

"Here is the giant *umiak*. The shaman was correct," Cikuq whispered. "And look: a second one."

Not one but two such *umiaks* lay icebound close to shore; the second vessel was not Raven's fabrication at all! This second *umiak* sat a short distance away from the first, listing toward the eastern sea. The boat leaned small and broken on its side, its hull caved in by ice and showing many splintered, brown antlers surrounding a gaping, shadowed hole.

"Turn, dogs!" Suddenly frightened, Kirima abruptly forced his sled around, backing his dogs toward the tundra to halt the team's progress. He set the snow hook as Gray Dog and his red companion whined and yipped in protestation, leaping against the tug lines. Cikuq followed Kirima's lead, stamping his own sled anchor deeply into the icy surface to secure his team. The dogs' whining increased as they pushed forward against the strength of Kirima's snow hook, their noses twitching in frustration that they could not investigate the strange scents hovering in the cold air.

Kirima ignored his team. Instead, he lifted his eyes to stare at the *umiak*.

Not even the shaman's description had prepared Kirima for the height of the antlers or the massive size of the intact vessel that towered above him, dark and imposing. The shadows cast by its enormous bulk reached out to the boy, the purple-gray fingers of the tall antlers pointing directly at his sled.

Have I ever seen such an enormous form? Not even the largest ice blocks tossed up on the shore during a storm compared to this.

The *umiak* creaked and groaned, and the boys exchanged frightened glances. Did the spirits of the Kabloonas inhabit these *umiaks*? Or did evil spirits dwell within?

The swirling wind that dispelled the earlier fog now whispered the shaman's words in Kirima's ears. *These men have powerful harpoons that sound like the sea ice breaking up in the spring. They are able to kill from a far distance.*

Kirima shuddered with dread. *What harm can they do to us and our dogs?*

Seeking reassurance, Kirima moved toward Cikuq, plucking at his sleeve, but the older boy remained frozen by his sled. Cikuq's dark eyes had filled with fear, and he pressed his lips firmly together as if to keep his chin from trembling.

Alarm squeezed Kirima's heart. *If Cikuq is afraid, we are lost. I need his courage not to fail.*

CRACK!

Both boys started violently as the second *umiak*'s hull snapped anew. As the ice squeezed the great *kayak*, the sharp report of the vessel's splintering frame echoed across the frozen land. The dying hull groaned as the *umiak*'s antlers listed farther toward the ice and the sagging lines slapped against its crumpling floor.

"Are we in danger?" Kirima turned to his companion. "Angakok said these men have harpoons that can reach as far as a white bear can swim."

But Cikuq did not answer.

Kirima trembled, his breath forming brief puffs in the frigid air. His heart struggled, caught between the determination to fulfill his destiny and the newly born fear that threatened to overtake his common sense.

He snuck a glance at his snow hook, still buried deeply in the ice. How easy it would be to release the hook in seconds and flee. He could sneak back toward the winter camp, away from the fearsome boats, away from their power and mystery, and most importantly, away from the ever-present menace of the white bear.

Then Kirima looked at Gray Dog, who was so willing to venture anywhere the boy asked. The boy sighed with love, chest filling with relief that he had not been forced to sacrifice his faithful sled dog. Then the sudden image of Qannik, snarling and barking as he leaped toward the white bear, flashed through Kirima's mind.

That was courage. That was the ultimate sacrifice.

Kirima raised his shoulders up to his ears and straightened his spine, dropping his shoulders and rotating them backward. His chest expanded as he took a deep breath.

My destiny is with these strange umiaks. *I am no coward. I will fulfill my promise to the People.*

As if in accord with Kirima, his dogs shuffled in their traces, ears pricked forward, eyes gazing intently toward the giant boats. They lifted their muzzles, two sets of black noses twitching, as they inhaled the unfamiliar scents in the distance.

Then Gray Dog lifted his nose toward the sky, the corners of his mouth beginning to form a howl of greeting.

"Quiet!" Kirima quickly grabbed the dog around his muzzle and forced him to the ground. Gray Dog lay down in the snow and put his chin on his paws in acquiescence.

"You hush, too," Kirima shushed Red Dog by shaking her snout gently. "And keep the gray one quiet."

Cikuq remained unmoving, clutching the handle of his sled. Kirima, still gazing at the strange wooden vessels, knelt by his team as another crack broke the silence. The ice squeezed the second *umiak*'s hull like the jaws of the great bear crushing the skull of a ringed seal.

We are not lost. We will not fail, Kirima thought. *I have courage for both of us.*

Rising, Kirima cleared his throat and put his hand on Cikuq's shoulder. "Let us gather our courage thick about us like a bearskin taken in deep winter. We must watch and wait until it is safe to go even closer."

Cikuq shook himself as a dog shakes water from his coat, then nodded. "Perhaps the goddess will now give us a sign of how to proceed."

No one stirred on the closer of the two boats, but it did not look abandoned. Boot tracks circled both vessels, and the skins hanging from the tall antlers of the closer *umiak* looked fresh against the sky. Some of these skins were furled along poles as long as many bear leg bones lashed together. Several parkas, all the color of the summer sky, flapped in the breeze; a thin thread of smoke arose from a square, wooden *iglu* on the *umiak*'s floor. An air of expectation surrounded this great *kayak*.

When no activity was forthcoming, Cikuq motioned toward the beach behind them. Following his older companion, Kirima took Red Dog's collar, and peering over their shoulders to make sure the Kabloonas had not spotted them, the boys ran their teams back up the beach toward a stretch of uplifted ice, where they would be hidden from view.

Despite the *umiaks*, Kirima's fear of Nanuq was still acute, and as the boys made camp, he carefully positioned himself downwind from the shore. This would allow his dogs to warn him if they scented any approaching bears. Neither boy made a fire to melt drinking water; smoke could alert any possible inhabitants of the *umiak* to the boys' presence. Instead, they slaked their thirst with snow thawed in seal bladders held next to their bare bellies.

They spent another long day awaiting a sign, with little to do but tell stories and reminisce about their life in the winter camps of their youth. When dusk fell, Cikuq, Kirima, and the dogs ate cold, raw duck. Worn out by boredom and discouragement, the companions did not attempt to make further conversation.

Long before nightfall, Kirima unhitched his dogs from their tug lines and pulled them toward him for warmth. Red Dog shoved her face against his chest and wagged her tail. Then she dropped one shoulder and lay down, snuggling close to her human partner. Gray Dog stepped on Kirima's outstretched legs, proceeded to walk across the boy's chest, and then flopped down on the empty place next to Kirima' ribs. The dog huffed and chuffed, wriggling until he was comfortable.

"Gray one," Kirima said, a hint of laughter in his voice despite the seriousness of the day. "You are as difficult a bed partner as Red Dog is an easy one!"

Tongue lolling, Gray Dog jumped up, play bowing before going through the entire bedtime ritual again. Kirima smiled again, and even Cikuq roused himself from his reverie to chuckle.

The tension broken at last, Kirima addressed Cikuq. "Where are the Kabloonas?" he asked.

Cikuq shook his head with a shrug and burrowed deeper into his bearskin rug.

Shivering slightly, Kirima covered himself with his bearskin and mulled over the mystery. He shook his foot free of the bearskin and reached over to jab his companion's sled.

"But Cikuq, what are they?" he persisted, questions tumbling from his mouth. "Are they fierce like the white bear? Or could Angakok be mistaken, and they are peaceable like the People ourselves? And when will we know what to do?"

"You are too impulsive, Kirima," Cikuq mumbled. "Remember, we must wait for a sign. We will not rush out to an uncertain fate." The older boy turned over and was soon snoring softly under his own bearskin rug.

Kirima sighed. *How can he sleep at a time like this?* Grudgingly, though, he agreed with his companion. Any impulsive act could indeed bring him to danger's door; he must prepare himself to wait. Perhaps a sign would be forthcoming soon.

As the sun slid into the ocean, streaking the gray-purple evening sky with yellow and gold, darkness slowly spread over the land. Kirima pulled his bearskin up to his chin. His heart beat forcefully as he pictured the enormity of their discovery: the two *umiaks*, captured by the ice.

"I will not lose my nerve. I will not be like my father," Kirima whispered to his sleeping dogs, setting his jaw and grasping Red Dog to his chest.

Roused, Red Dog stretched her muzzle upward and gave Kirima two small licks on his chin. The stars twinkled above as she watched over him, and soon, Kirima slipped deep into slumber.

Some time later, the dogs woke Kirima as they freed themselves from the boy's grasp. Tails waving, they walked to the end of their tethers and dug matching shelters in the drift snow on the leeward side of the sled. Settling in, they sighed and began to lick their feet, cleaning off the duck blood that had stained them during their evening meal. Unable to return to sleep, Kirima uncovered his head and gazed up as the Northern Lights danced above, eclipsing the stars and sending curtains of red and green across the night sky.

Were his ancestors among the lights, playing kickball with a walrus skull? And did his other, more ancient ancestors hold up colored torches to light the path of the spirits of the newly dead?

A strange, otherworldly sensation overcame Kirima suddenly; he was aware that he was neither fully conscious nor near the edge of sleep. Then, as he watched the lights flare and shimmer, the image of a great sun loomed red in the dark, glimmering intensely in the sky. The sun throbbed as if expanding and contracting, and reflexively, Kirima laid his hand on his heart. The image of the sun pulsed with the same cadence as his own heartbeat. A single set of human footprints wound their way around the pulsating sun.

"This is my sign," Kirima whispered. "I am like the sun, a traveler in a strange land. In my dream quest, the sun goddess has shown me what to do."

Resolve filled Kirima's heart. The boy could finally relax; he allowed his eyes to close with weariness. As he drowsed, his grandmother's voice spoke in his dreams, telling the story of Malina, the sun goddess.

Malina lived with her brother, Anningan. The two spent their childhood playing games, but when their childhood ended, their life together changed.

One day, the two had a disagreement, and in anger, Anningan attacked his sister. During the fight, a seal oil lamp overturned, spilling oil on Malina's hands.

When she pushed Anningan away, Malina spread dirty, black oil over her brother's face. So angered was Anningan that Malina fled in fear and ran as far as she could into the sky, where she became the sun. Anningan pursued her and became the moon.

To this day, Anningan remains angry that oil was smeared over him, and he often forgets to eat, becoming thinner as the days go by. Every month, the moon disappears for a long sleep while Anningan finally eats. Then, growing in size once more, he remembers his anger and returns to chase his sister again. This eternal chase makes the sun alternate with the moon in the sky.

Rousing himself, Kirima blinked up at the sky. Anningan was only as big as the end of the boy's thumb nail; the starving time in the sky echoed this season on Earth. Then Kirima closed his eyes again and slept.

Dawn found Cikuq snoring as Kirima hastily fed the four dogs choice pieces of duck meat. His vision had indicated he must go on foot to the *umiaks*; the dogs would remain here. But seeing the dogs strain against their collars, the boy glanced at his sled's snow hook. Had he planted it firmly enough into the hard ice?

"I should have brought a piece of antler with me," he said to his dogs as he tamped the hook further through the frozen surface. "Then I could have made my dogs fast like Baral showed me."

Testing the hook, he tugged the dogs' harness lines, verifying that the sled was secure. The hook seemed well anchored, but still it wiggled; the boy would take no chances. Kirima stamped on his snow hook again, sending a quick prayer to the spirits of the wind that the hook would hold.

The time to follow his destiny had come. Kirima jiggled Cikuq's shoulder, interrupting the older boy's snores.

"The sign came to me as a large red sun, shining through the Northern Lights and surrounded by footprints," he began. "I believe it was sent by the sun goddess, telling me to go alone, on foot, to the *umiak* to see what I can do to restore the whales and seals to our shores."

These words brought Cikuq fully awake. He rubbed his eyes. "You saw a great red sun in your dreams? Are you sure this sign was meant for you alone? Perhaps I am to go as well."

Kirima shook his head emphatically. "I saw only a single set of footprints. You must remain here. If there is danger, one of us must stay alive to bring news of the other back to our families."

Deep furrows creased Cikuq's forehead. "If there is danger, two of us can face it better than one alone. Did we not agree we are stronger together?"

Kirima shook his head again. "No. The sun goddess sent the sign to me alone. You will be needed here to feed the dogs and keep them from their own foolishness."

Kirima's voice was quiet, but the new tone in his voice brought Cikuq's head up. Recognizing the unfamiliar resolve in his friend's voice, the older boy searched Kirima's face. He then nodded slowly.

"Do not be gone longer than it takes to butcher a caribou bull," Cikuq said. "If you do not return, I will come find you."

With a half-grin, Cikuq nodded in parting, watching with reluctance as Kirima jogged off in the direction of the great *umiaks*.

Just as Kirima descended the sloping ice leading to the edge of the sea, all four dogs sent up a cacophony of howls. The snapping of sinew as the dogs leaped against their tethers accentuated their howls and barks of protest; they did not want to be left behind.

Kirima's lingering fears flickered as Cikuq quieted their teams, and the boy scanned the shore and sea ice for the distinctive shape of Nanuq.

I will ask Father's spirit to keep the great bear from stalking me on this ice shelf.

Kirima lowered his voice to show his courage and called up the slope. "Do not hush the dogs! They will warn us if any bears are nearby."

Then Kirima resumed hiking along the pressure ridge, drawing closer to the strange *umiaks*. He kept one ear focused behind him, listening for the dogs. When he reached the shore, he crouched behind a tall block of ice and peered over the top.

Then he recalled Cikuq's advice. *If this hunter were a white bear sneaking up on a seal, he would cover his black nose so the seal could not see him against the white snow.* Thankful once again for his companion's knowledge and guidance, Kirima pulled up the hood of his parka, hiding his dark hair.

The young Inuk turned his attention toward the sea and examined the closest *umiak*.

The frozen water has clasped its arms tightly around that strange hull, and the second one has almost disappeared into the ice. Do these Kabloonas not understand the nature of the northern sea when spring is unfaithful and dances with winter after her return to the land?

He crouched, hidden, while he contemplated how to approach the larger of the two *umiaks*. *Where are the men the shaman said lived upon this strange boat?*

As if in answer, two men appeared from a doorway on the *umiak*, staggering and gesticulating. Kirima started in astonishment, and his eyes widened. At last, here they were—the Kabloonas! And no wonder Angakok called them "Cloud Men"—their hair was indeed like dried grass, their skin the color of clouds.

But that was not all. One of the men was short and stocky, like an Inuit man, but unlike an Inuk, a dense, reddish beard covered this Kabloona's chin and upper lip. The second man was tall, very tall, with long, shoulder-length hair that glowed yellowish in the morning sun. In his hand, he carried a long stick the color of the sea on a cloudy day.

As Kirima drew closer, he made out the details of the clothing the men wore. And what strange clothing indeed! Instead of hairy caribou parkas, the men were clad in a type of flat skin, blue like the sky at nightfall, the color of no animal the boy could imagine. Down the front of each parka, bright buttons glinted in the morning twilight. The taller of the two wore a hat not of animal fur, but of the same blue skins making up his coat. The sound of the men's angry voices as they argued in their guttural language carried easily across the sea ice.

How can they communicate with such ugly sounds?

Without warning, the men started to scuffle, swinging their fists as they bellowed like bull walruses in the breeding season. The bearded man ran forward, grabbing the long stick from the tall man before pointing it at him. The tall man feinted around his adversary, swinging what looked to Kirima like a piece of tubular ice that glinted in the early morning light. He struck the bearded one on his head and then gave him a mighty shove. The stricken man tumbled gracelessly over the edge of the *umiak* and, still holding the stick, landed with a thud on the ice far below. The tall man threw the tube of ice overboard, shouting and shaking his fist at the one on the ice.

Still crouching in his hiding place, Kirima put his own fist to his chest to calm his rapidly beating heart. *These men have no manners! Do they not value peace above all else?* Perhaps the bearded man lying on the ice once laughed with the other man's wife without permission. Or perhaps one of the men had angered Sedna and endangered the entire *umiak* village. Approaching the giant *kayak* and hailing the strangers might be unwise after all.

140

The man on the ice lay still, then slowly rolled over and climbed to his knees. Blood ran down the side of his face. He crawled to the tube, tipping it up and holding it to his mouth. With a cry of disappointment, he flung it away and gathered up the long stick. Unable to balance, he weaved and reeled, carving meandering footprints in the snow that lightly covered the ice sheet.

This man is land-sick!

The boy himself had experienced this once, when after a long day in his father's *kayak* in rough water, Kirima could not balance after coming ashore. And when he had returned to his father's snow house afterward, the walls of the *iglu* seemed to move to the rhythm of the sea swells.

Holding his head, the land-sick Kabloona shouted upward at his companion, but his cries went unheeded as the other man dismissed him with a gesture of disdain. Shaking his fist at the man above, the bearded man stumbled and almost fell again. He walked to the piece of tubular ice and picked it up, slipping it into the pocket of his parka. Then, to Kirima's surprise, the man struck out across the ice shelf, heading away from the *umiak* toward the shore.

Where is he going? He has no dogsled to take him inland to build a shelter. He has no hood to keep his head from sending his body heat into the sky. All he has is a long stick and a tube of ice. He will perish.

But the man did not travel very far. He stopped, bent over, and vomited before taking a few hesitant steps in Kirima's direction. Then, as quickly as the hunter drops a caribou with a spear to the heart, the man fell face forward onto the ice and was still.

The sun rose in the sky as indecision plagued the Inuit boy. His body became overheated as he fretted about his next move, so he removed his heavy gloves and outer parka to keep from breaking out in a sweat. He folded the coat in half and sat on it, watching the man on the ice for signs of life.

Surely the stranger's companion will come for him now, Kirima thought. He looked toward the wooden *umiak,* then at the fallen man, and then toward the *umiak* again. But the other Kabloona did not come to the man's aid.

Should he himself approach? And what should he do once he came near to the bearded Cloud Man? Kirima bit his lower lip with uncertainty.

At last, Kirima decided to act. *This stranger may be on a journey to the spirit world. I am the only one who can help Cloud Man. The goddess of the sea would be angry if this hunter allowed him to die. And I have not heard the dogs howling—both the goddess and my ancestors must be protecting me from Nanuq.*

Heartened, Kirima shook the stiffness from his legs, touched the bear claw hanging around his neck, and put his parka and gloves back on. Then he crept toward the fallen man softly and gently, putting each hand and knee carefully on the snow-crusted ice to silence the sound of his approach.

I must do what I can to keep the stranger on this side of life. If this strange man's soul leaves his body in anger, it will bring bad fortune to everyone on this part of the ice shelf. And if I save a life such as this, this Kabloona's spirit may allow the seals to reach the People.

As Kirima continued creeping forward, the weight he had been carrying, a weight as large as a musk ox's head, lifted from his heart. He inhaled deeply, letting his breath out with a long sigh. *At last I have found my destiny!*

Reaching the stranger at last, Kirima knelt beside the unconscious man. Then, grunting with effort, the boy rolled the Kabloona over onto his back. A small section of the man's cheek remained frozen to the ice; Kirima winced as the patch of skin tore from the stranger's face with a small ripping sound. Using his outer glove to stem the flow of blood, the boy put pressure on the man's wound. The blood from the gash on the man's head slowly congealed on the ice.

The Kabloona was breathing. The boy could do little for him here in the rising wind, with no food and no way to build a shelter. Kirima glanced at the *umiak,* again hoping that help was forthcoming, but the boat's floor remained empty. He and the strange man were alone.

Still, his curiosity overwhelmed him. Kirima removed his blood-crusted glove and reached out to touch the stranger's clothing. He marveled at the feel of the man's jacket, rough and scratchy under his hand. He was almost as captivated by the color of the parka as he was curious about the color of the man's skin. *Parka the color of the sky just before night falls. Face the color of the summer clouds.*

Then he picked up the man's large, heavy stick and examined the shaft closely. He tapped on the shiny end, startled to hear a hollow ping float through the air. How hard the stick was! And how cold!

"This stick is not made from antler or driftwood," he murmured. "The shaft is harder than wood and is the color of the darkened sea when snow falls."

The Kabloona stirred when the boy spoke, but quickly slid back to unconsciousness.

"Cloud Man," Kirima said to the inert figure, "the wind has risen. You are safe here, but not for long. I will hurry, and my traveling companion and I will bring the dogs and a sled to take you back to camp and keep you warm."

He set the mysterious stick down next to Cloud Man. "Your people are angry people and may not allow you to live if I take you back to your *umiak,*" he continued. "I will care for you and ask the spirits to return life to your body."

Leaving Cloud Man behind for the moment, Kirima hurried back to the makeshift camp.

But an unsettling quiet met him as he strode into camp. Cikuq was gone!

Cikuq's sled and dog team were gone, too. Furthermore, no Red Dog rose to greet the boy, *wooing* her soft welcome. No Gray Dog sat up, scratching at his shoulder with his hind foot to ease the itchy spot where his harness rubbed. All the dogs had disappeared. Only Kirima's sled remained. The blowing snow had covered whatever tracks might have remained.

Kirima raised his gaze to the barren snowscape around the camp. No dogs in the distance, no dots on the horizon. The ice shelf was as silent as a stillborn caribou.

Eee-yi! Kirima cried to himself. *No Cikuq! Where is he? And no dogs! When did they free themselves? I thought they were fast!*

Frantically, he lifted his hands to shade his eyes and scanned the ice shelf all the way to the distant shoreline. No dogs, bobbing up and down as they ran, interrupted the outline of the flat horizon. No sign of Cikuq looming into view on his sled, and the snow had obliterated the older boy's sled trail, too.

Just one piece of antler would have anchored the dogs!

Sick at heart, Kirima gathered up his bearskin bed and bundled it back into his sled bag. Resigned, he strapped the gang line around his shoulders and, dragging his sled, trudged over the ice toward Cloud Man.

Two men against the arctic cold are better than one. I must keep Cloud Man on this side of the spirit world. He bit his lower lip to keep his chin from quivering. *Now is the time for courage, so I may continue as the sun goddess directed. But what will I do without my dogs?*

As he skirted a block of upthrust sea ice and skittered down across the uneven surface, the boy closed his eyes in anguish. He had not planned well enough for this trip. His heart on fire with the shaman's words, he had raced off without listening to his head. In his haste, and despite his resolve to miss nothing, he had not packed the antler anchor or checked for his *pilaut*. And Cikuq had fled the camp—had he met with some dire misfortune? Now, alone on the ice shelf with no dogs, he and Cloud Man might be doomed to freeze or starve.

At last he approached the pressure ridge just beyond which Cloud Man lay. Kirima dropped the shoulder lines and climbed over the last of the ridge unencumbered. Below, the stranger still lay face up, the fine snow blowing over him as his mottled hands idly plucked at his parka buttons.

Kirima approached with slow, measured steps, holding out his hands in appeasement. Kabloonas had shown themselves to be angry men, and Kirima was not sure how Cloud Man would react to seeing an Inuk nearby.

The snow shushed beneath Cloud Man's head as he turned toward the boy. His unfocused eyes darted back and forth under their puffy lids.

Kirima knelt beside the stranger, lifting him into a sitting position. The man did not protest, so Kirima dragged him by his collar back to the sled. He rolled Cloud Man into the sled basket and covered him with the bearskin. Panting, the young Inuk rested until his heartbeat returned to normal. Then Kirima picked up the man's heavy stick and retrieved the ice tube as well, marveling now at its cold hardness and translucent finish.

Kirima slipped his shoulders back into the traces of his sled and leaned into the makeshift harness. The boy needed most of his strength to pull Cloud Man over the icy ridges of the ice shelf and back to camp. There, he scanned from horizon to horizon for any sign of Cikuq, the dogs, or Nanuq. This was the season of mother bears and their cubs, and a mother bear would not hesitate to attack even a full-grown male bear to defend her family.

The landscape remained empty; only the blowing snow offered relief from the barrenness of the ice shelf.

Relieved that at least no bears were near, Kirima tipped Cloud Man out of the sled, turning it on its side to create a shelter from the ever-present wind. Then he made a bed with the bearskin and tucked it all around Cloud Man. The stranger did not stir.

Grateful that the last of the duck meat remained safely buried in their snowy cache and had not disappeared with Cikuq and the dogs, Kirima went about melting snow and thawing the meat for their evening meal. Cloud Man was unable to eat, but he roused himself enough to swallow a few sips of life-sustaining water. Then his eyes rolled back as he quickly returned to the land between this and the spirit world.

Kirima made his own bed, burrowing next to Cloud Man for warmth as he fell into an uneasy slumber, visions of white bears stalking him across the empty ice shelf warring with visions of Cikuq being attacked by Nanuq.

The Northern Lights brought with them a fierce cold, and when Cloud Man began shaking, Kirima jolted awake.

"Do not go shivering into the darkness of the spirit world!" Kirima cried out, seizing Cloud Man's arm. The stranger simply blinked his eyes, almost too deep in cold to react.

I must not panic! Kirima took deep breaths to calm himself. What had Baral taught him about being caught in the cold with no dogs for warmth?

I will never again complain about Baral's instruction, Kirima thought with gratitude.

The boy rose and began banking snow around the sled, chinking it thoroughly to keep out the night wind. He emptied his sled bag and partially detached it from the sled, propping it over Cloud Man's head and shoulders before then driving his long spear into the snow at an angle steep enough to hold up the bag. This makeshift shelter would help contain what-

146

ever warm air their breath generated, keeping it from escaping quickly into the night sky. Finally, Kirima removed his own clothing, and shivering and bare-skinned, undressed Cloud Man as well. Then he rolled up both himself and the stranger together in the bear rug, skin to skin, and drew the rug over their heads.

Kirima tucked Cloud Man's hands into his own armpits, shuddering at the shock of cold, and put his arms around the stranger.

I wish I had retrieved my scraps of fox fur from the sled! But it was too cold to go in search of additional coverings for their feet. To lose one's toes to the cold was not as serious as losing one's fingers.

They passed the night in misery, the glacial breath of the ice shelf chilling them each time either of them moved. Beset by dread, Kirima slept little, listening in vain for the sound of Cikuq returning and thinking only of a way to survive without his dogs.

Chapter 10

The following morning, just at dawn, Kirima dressed hastily and rolled out of his sleeping skin. He melted snow in his seal bladder, flinching as it touched his bare belly. He then rolled the bladder under Cloud Man's arm to keep the water from freezing again before carefully re-tucking the bearskin around his naked body. The Kabloona stirred, snoring for a few breaths, but did not waken.

Kirima's stomach grumbled in hungry protest as he scanned the horizon. No storm clouds gathered in the distance; the wind had traveled to distant lands. This was fine weather for hunting seals. Gathering his hunting gear from his sled bag, Kirima wrinkled his brow. Where was his short sealing spear? The boy searched among his possessions, but his sealing spear was not there. Kirima sat back on his heels, scratching his head. First his *pilaut,* and now—Yutu! The bully had taken Kirima's sealing spear, too!

No dogs, no friend, no knife, and now no sealing harpoon. All I have is a snow knife and a long whaling harpoon. How will I kill a seal with those? How will I butcher it? How will I survive?

Not ready to give up, Kirima looked about him for a sign. The sun's rays glinted off the ice crust, sending shards of light into the air, turning blood red as the sun rose above the horizon. *The sun! Here is my signal again!*

Kirima squared his shoulders. *I have faith that the goddess will send game that I can kill with my whaling harpoon. I will survive somehow.*

He took a deep breath. The time was ripe to hunt. At least he still had his long spear and *pana*. Setting off toward the shore, he raised his eyes to the heavens, sending a prayer to the sea goddess.

Perhaps she will smile on me this day. After all, the seals were among Sedna's first gifts.

As he walked, Kirima remembered the story of the coming of the seals to the arctic. In the very beginning of time, a group of Inuit had set out on the sea to find food. They had only one *kayak* and found there was not room for everyone. So a girl, brought along to learn how to butcher the seal, was pushed overboard. Desperately, she clung to the sides of the vessel, but she had no relatives in the *kayak* to protect her. One of the hunters cut off her fingers, and the girl fell, drifting to the bottom of the sea. One finger became a seal, one became a whale, one became a walrus, and one became a salmon. The girl herself became the Sedna, sea goddess, who henceforward would create all the animals of the sea.

As the sun rose higher in the sky, Kirima sang a song to Sedna:

> *Sedna, goddess of all sea creatures, goddess of all life*
> *Send me a seal. Send me a sea bird. Send me some food.*
> *Make my aim true. Make my aim strong.*
> *I praise the sea, the sky, the land for their bounty*
> *I praise the seals for their courage.*
> *I praise the birds for their beauty.*
> *Sedna, I sing to the land, the sea, and the sky.*
> *Sedna, I sing to all your creatures,*
> *Sedna, I sing to you.*

Kirima sang with hope in his head, but the remnants of foreboding remained in his heart. *How am I to survive if the goddess is angry? How will I stay alive without the knowledge and skill of Cikuq? Without the warmth and power of my dogs? How will I keep Cloud Man on this side of the spirit world? How will I fulfill my quest?*

Kirima crested a short upslope, then halted. A dark shape sprawled on the ice before him. As he drew near, the shape transformed into a partially eaten ringed seal, head and body gone, but with some of the innards still intact, lying in a pool of frozen blood.

With a sharp intake of breath and a wide grin, he rejoiced. *My luck has turned!*

The scuff marks of a medium-sized white bear, likely a female, and those of a much smaller one surrounded the seal; the faint but discernible imprints indicated a scuffle between the two. A youngster, probably an adolescent male, must have tried to wrest the seal from its mother, but for some reason, the two had abandoned the remains and fled inland. But what had sent the bears away from their meal?

Kirima cast about and soon discovered the reason the two bears took flight.

Eee-yi! Here a male bear came to the breathing hole.

The male Nanuq was the only enemy of a mother bear and her cub; such a one would kill and eat both if he could.

I will not panic! I will investigate to see what might have happened.

The boy hunkered down and put his hands into the great depressions the bear's paws made in the snow. The outline of the bear's claws was clear in the sunlight.

Here he started to run toward the seal. The tracks are deep. The prints lie on top of the others. And here, he stole the seal.

Kirima's eyes followed the mother and cub's tracks inland. The two had fled before the male reached them, and the male bear's tracks led away from the kill, following the mother and her baby.

I hope the big male has eaten his fill and his stomach does not tell him to return to this kill.

But this was not the time to panic. Kirima examined the remains of the seal, concentrating hard on the task of obtaining food. Most of the seal had disappeared into the bears' stomachs, leaving only a scrap of hide, some intestines, a little meat, and a smear of blubber, as well as the bladder which lay frozen to the bloody snow. The boy walked about, searching for the liver, but it was gone.

I hope the bear appeased the goddess when it ate this important liver.

Still, Sedna had smiled upon him. He sang a song of thanks to the sea goddess for bringing him to this place at this time. Then, using his *pana*, Kirima scraped the meat and blubber from the seal hide and ate it. He then sucked and chewed on the bloody hide, gleaning every trace of nourishment from the remains of the seal. Lingering, however, was unwise, so as he chewed, Kirima used his snow knife to pry the seal's bladder from the ice. He cut a slit in the bladder and emptied it. After cleansing it thoroughly with snow, he painstakingly scraped the bloody snow into the bladder, packing it tight. Then he poked the remains of the blubber into the bladder, and holding the bladder next to his skin to melt the icy blood, he turned toward camp.

As he trudged across the snow, the boy's worries about Nanuq resurfaced. He glanced over his shoulder, searching for the bear. Despite his determination not to fear the great beast, his heart began to pound. *Listen to your head!* Kirima removed the bladder from within his parka, clenching and unclenching his hands as he shifted the bladder from one hand to the other.

The big bear is gone. He hunts the cub. He will not return for me.

His pace deliberate, Kirima followed his own faint tracks back toward the camp. But he could not keep himself from looking up repeatedly, searching for any moving shapes that stood out against the stillness of the landscape.

O Father, how I wish you were here to give me courage!

Finally, when no threatening silhouettes broke the smooth edges of the horizon, he looked to the vast beach beyond, hoping to catch a glimpse of two small shapes, one red and one gray, playing in the cold. But he remained alone on the ice shelf with no dogs, no Cikuq, and only a sick and disabled Cloud Man for company.

Kirima proceeded back to camp, led by the lick of a sea breeze on the side of his face and the vague imprint of his tracks that had all but disappeared. The horizon was indistinct, a white blur with no demarcation between land and sky. By the time he arrived, the wind had picked up again, and its icy breath was strong enough to push the hood of his parka over his eyes.

The winter wind has fought with the new spring and gained power over the land again. This man must rebuild the shelter so the cold will not throw its deadly cloak over the man from the great umiak.

Quickly, he checked on Cloud Man. Though deep in sleep with no sign of waking, the Kabloona was alive. The stranger had even summoned enough energy to dress himself, and that gratified Kirima.

Kirima began rummaging through his equipment for his caribou shoulder bone shovel. *A big wind is coming. We must have deep shelter. The snow here is not the snow for making ice blocks.*

Finding the shovel, Kirima dug a deep trench the length of his sled. He woke Cloud Man and motioned him to roll out from the shelter of the sled. The Kabloona obliged, heaving himself onto the trampled snow next to the sled. Grunting with effort, Kirima dragged the sled into the trench; this would keep the sled, basket and all, upright on its side. With the shovel, he dug out the snow in front of the sled, chipping down into the ice and creating a deep depression in the ground. The work brought heat to the boy's body, and to cool himself, he withdrew the thawed seal bladder from his parka. He packed it next to Cloud Man, letting the stranger's body heat keep it from freezing solid again.

Where is Cikuq? Is he still alive? Will we ever meet again as Inuit men on this side of the spirit world? Kirima's stomach began to ache with dread and grief. *How will I find words to tell his family that he is gone?*

Cloud Man roused himself and rolled over to lean on one arm, panting slightly in the cold air and watching Kirima with heavy eyelids. The stranger pulled himself up and tried to kneel, but fell back again, groaning. He glanced down at the bulge of the bladder under his parka, touching it inquiringly, but soon lost interest. He placed his hands on either side of his forehead and pressed. Kirima looked at him, his brow furrowed but his eyes full of compassion.

The blow on his head has made Cloud Man head sick. He is in too much pain to help himself.

By the time Kirima had dug a satisfactory snow cave, the temperature had dropped and the wind moaned, whipping ice particles painfully against his exposed face and ears. Quickly, he pulled his parka hood over his head and remade their bed, using his insulating walrus and fox skins as a ground cover under the bear rug. He moved to the windward side of the sled and covered it firmly with the snow. His legs shook from fatigue, and now hunger gnawed at his stomach, joining the ache of dread and grief. His lips became stiff and his teeth clacked against each other as his body was wracked with shivers.

Kirima quickly settled himself in the shelter next to Cloud Man, feeling the Kabloona's warmth penetrate his own freezing body. The boy took the seal bladder from under Cloud Man's coat and pantomimed drinking from it before holding it to the other man's mouth. Cloud Man took a sip, grimaced, and spit the seal blood out, rolling away and covering his head with the bearskin. Kirima drank the blood with relish, feeling its power course through his body. Some of his tiredness dropped away, and his shivering abated. He nudged his companion and rubbed his own stomach, using gestures in an effort to coax Cloud Man to eat some of the seal blubber, but the stranger turned away again, holding his head at the temples.

The fierce storm kept the two in their snow cave for the rest of that day and into the night. Kirima and Cloud Man passed the time bundled together in an uncomfortable silence, waiting for the storm to pass. Kirima rationed the bloody snow inside the bladder, taking only a small amount more that day, for the two could well be pinned in the cave for days on end. The boy's father had once passed down the story of an Inuit hunting party who had not survived a great storm even after sacrificing their dogs. Stranded for sleeps past counting, they had eaten their fill. But when the dog meat was gone, the sudden lack of food and the cold had taken their deadly toll on the hunters. These were foolish hunters, his father had said; the wise Inuk knew to eat only small amounts of food daily, for that told the body to conserve energy.

But both Kirima and Cloud Man grew markedly weaker as the storm raged. When the wind finally abated, the stranger was ready to drink the last of the seal blood; though he still grimaced at the taste, the drink revived the pale-skinned man enough to sit up unaided. The cold had not lessened, however, and when Cloud Man began shivering again, Kirima made yellow water into his two seal bladders and packed them in the stranger's armpits for warmth.

"I could trade parkas with you, Cloud Man," Kirima said. "Yours may not keep you warm enough to survive. But if I cannot stay warm in your clothing, then both of us will cross the barrier between this world and the next."

The words hung in the air, and Cloud Man simply turned away from the boy, put his head down, and slept.

"Cikuq is gone," Kirima mumbled. "I have no dogs to keep us warm." His shivering began anew, fear licking at his heart as he considered their predicament. *No meat, no blubber, only slightly warm water in these seal bladders. What am I to do? Where is my courage, my determination?*

Late into the night, the stars shone with an unnatural intensity. Exhausted by worry and fear, Kirima finally slept.

Calm descended on the camp as the stars turned to greet the morning, their luster fading in the early light. The dawn was clear, but Kirima did not stir until the clasp of night loosened its icy hold on the land. Then he inched back the bearskin and looked at the sky. If he could, he should make water again for Cloud Man's seal bladders, but a strange lassitude had overcome the boy.

I do not want to move, he thought. *I am no longer shivering, for this bearskin nest is almost warm. My thirst has gone, and my stomach has stopped begging for meat.*

His heart beat wildly as his thoughts became a confusion of images, both past and present. Kirima's mind drifted to other days, other times. There was Qannik, his white sled dog, napping in the sun. Cloud Man's face transformed itself into that of his father, ghostly pale in the light of his shelter. Had his father, indeed, come back to Earth to comfort him?

"Father?" Kirima spoke hoarsely, his voice growing weak. "Father?"

Cloud Man stirred, and his recumbent form transformed to a pile of fluffy hair. Why, the caribou had come! They were shedding their winter coats in preparation for summer! Kirima peeked across the bearskin covering and reached out, intending to pluck a handful of the matted undercoat. Then his hand dropped to his side.

Oh, he was so warm! He must take off his parka and trousers. Kirima grasped the hem of his parka, but his clumsy fingers lacked the strength to pull it over his head. The boy gave up and leaned against Cloud Man's hip. He closed his eyes against the pain beginning to throb behind his eyelids.

How tired he was, so very tired. Could he simply slip into the warmth of his bearskin and sleep forever? How easily he could surrender his spirit to the goddess, to float amongst the stars, free of the body wracked with the pain of cold, hunger, and fatigue. How warm would be the tenderness of her embrace. He had only to give in to this welcoming lethargy. How easy it would be.... Kirima sighed deeply. His head nodded, and he rolled over onto his side, covering his head with the bearskin.

Father, you are near. I feel your presence. Have you come to take me to the Great Village in the sky?

A loud huffing broke through to Kirima's consciousness. He roused himself enough to hear rough, uneven panting from the other side of the sled. His lassitude dropped away as fear stabbed his heart.

Nanuq! The great bear had hunted them in the storm's aftermath!

The rush of terror renewed Kirima's spirit, clearing his head. He squirmed away from Cloud Man. His heart pounded and the palms of his hands glistened as the cold bit him once again. Stealthily, he grabbed his long spear and, quaking, turned slowly toward the sound.

Huff, huff! Grrrrr...HUFF!

Terror clawed at Kirima's heart. Nanuq!

Kirima changed his grip on the long spear so he could sidle out of the shelter. Once again praying to his father for courage, he crawled from under the sled bag and crept around the end of the sled, positioning himself below the mound of snow that held the sled in its trench.

How huge was the bear? How hungry? How fierce?

Coming to his knees, he raised his head inch by inch above the snow mounded around the shelter sides. Though he trembled so violently that his spear rattled against the sled runner, he gathered his courage and slowly peeked over the edge.

Then, astonished, Kirima stood upright. "*Pah!*"

In front of Kirima stood Cikuq and his team. He led more two dogs, a red one and a gray one, harnesses intact, but tug lines hopelessly tangled, and both grinning and panting as they scratched themselves in the morning sun. Between them, guarded by the red husky, five fat lemmings lay on the ground.

"The dogs ran off!" Cikuq said. "I followed their trail and found them just before the wind covered their tracks. And see what they have caught for us to eat!"

Kirima stood immobile, mouth hanging open while Cikuq unhitched his dog team, grinning back over his shoulder at his companion.

Kirima dropped his harpoon as the fear drained from his body. His neck and shoulders, stiff with tension, relaxed. His legs could no longer support him, and he collapsed in the churned-up snow, leaning against the back of the half-buried sled.

"I thought you had travelled to the land of the spirits! I thought I was alone!"

Kirima cuffed Red Dog, then gathered her up in his arms. She wriggled in an ecstasy of greeting, twisting around to lick his face. Kirima kicked one of the lemmings with his sealskin boot.

"Oh, you dogs!" Kirima yelled, half in fury and half in relief. "You think you can appease me by bringing back food!" But he spoke with laughter, for the gift had indeed appeased him.

He ran his hands across their ribs and smiled. "You have fattened up, you bad wolves. And decided to feed me, too! These Inuuk will eat lemmings!"

Gray Dog leaped up and jumped on the boy in greeting, shoving Red Dog out of Kirima's arms. Kirima stumbled backwards, fell, and was immediately engulfed by fur and tongues and waving tails.

Energized by relief and no longer cold to the point of death, the boy extricated himself from the dog pile and began to untangle the tug lines, whispering threats and reprimands under his breath.

Unabashed, Gray Dog trotted around the shelter to investigate the new scent in the air. Whining with excitement, he approached Cloud Man with wagging tail and prancing feet. Still attached to Gray Dog, Red Dog had no choice but to follow; her uplifted nose, however, showed her curiosity about the strange smell of this new man as well.

Warmed considerably by all the excitement, but still ravenously hungry, Kirima plunged through the soft snow, following his dogs.

Cloud Man, roused by the commotion, held his hand out to ward off Gray Dog's greeting.

"Get back!" Kirima shouted to the gray one, who was busy sniffing and snuffling every inch of the man in the bearskin.

Red Dog snarled at her furry companion, and Gray Dog retreated. Both dogs lay down in sight of Cloud Man, but Kirima's stern warning growl kept them from venturing closer to either the stranger or the lemmings.

"Is this a Kabloona from the *umiak*?" Cikuq stood above the prone figure, peering down in curiosity.

The older boy sat down next to the stranger, inching onto a corner of the bearskin rug. Cloud Man squinted into Cikuq's face, then closed his eyes and put his head down.

Cikuq took off his gloves and touched the Kabloona's hair and face. "Skin that feels like mine, but that looks like the white dawn. Hair the color of the tundra grass in the fall," he muttered.

Kirima put his hand on Cloud Man's shoulder to reassure him that

Cikuq meant no harm. "This is a man who I saw pushed off his *umiak* when he angered a fellow villager. He wandered alone across the ice shelf until I rescued him, but he is still sick from a blow to the head. I believe he will help us save the People. If we keep Cloud Man from death and send him back to his people, I think the goddess will smile on us and send seals and whales back to our shores."

His expression quizzical, Cikuq nodded. "Tie up your dogs, firmly this time. I will watch over this strange person."

Nodding, Kirima grabbed his dogs by their collars, holding them fast as he untangled their lines. "Stay!" he ordered, his booted feet scraping a trough in the ice several feet away from the sled. He laid the ends of the dogs' harness lines into the trough and made yellow water, covering the braided traces with the liquid. He waited patiently for the water to freeze over the braided caribou sinew, testing the strength of his dog anchor.

Content that his dogs were now held fast away from both the lemmings and Cloud Man, Kirima turned back to the Kabloona. The man was awake now, with Cikuq kneeling by his side.

I will bring Red Dog to warm this man, Kirima decided. He untied Red Dog from her tether and led her by her collar to the stranger. She sniffed Cloud Man's face and pawed at his arm, panting and waving her tail. Cloud Man, half-smiling, reached out to touch the fur under her chest.

"Red Dog will help keep him warm," Kirima said to Cikuq, gesturing for the red one to nestle next to the stranger. "He has been shivering, and I alone am not able to keep him warm enough to stay alive."

Cloud Man rolled toward the warmth of the grinning sled dog. After a few moments, his waxen cheeks flushed with a faint pink glow. His breathing was no longer so labored. He tried to sit up, but Red Dog's weight and his own weakness pulled him back down. Repositioning the dog, he managed to sit for a few moments before lying down again, but he stayed awake, watching the boys from under his puffy eyelids.

Confident that Cloud Man had returned to the world of the living, Kirima ate a bit of snow until his thirst was slaked. Hunger reawakened, he picked up the largest of the five lemmings and sniffed it. Despite his earlier enthusiasm, he made a face and turned it over in his hands.

"Have you eaten lemming?" he asked Cikuq.

Cikuq shook his head vigorously. "Our first taste of it was my only taste. I have never needed to eat a lemming. It is dog food." Cikuq wrinkled his upper lip in distaste. Then he sighed. "But we did try it once. And it is meat, after all. We all need meat."

"Perhaps it will taste better this time, like a duck or ptarmigan."

The boys had misgivings, but in desperation, Kirima picked up his *pana* and tried to butcher the lemmings. But his snow knife was too dull and unwieldy to finish the job. Oh, to have his *pilaut* instead!

Seeing his companion's struggle, Cikuq intervened, his *pilaut* ready. "You have worked hard enough," he said. "Let this lazy hunter do his share."

Kirima nodded his thanks. "This task was no match for a *pana*," he said.

The work finished, the boys laid the rodent meat out to cure in the sun. Cikuq handed a small liver to Kirima; tasting it, the boy found the flavor strangely bland but not at all unpleasant.

"Apak says that hunger will coax a man to eat things he does not think he can," Kirima said. "This liver is oily but not as bitter as I thought. Besides, the meat will keep us all from the spirit world."

The boys gave a prayer of thanks to the small animals that gave their lives so the Inuit boys might live. They shared some of the meat, each hesitating before the first bite, then smiled through blood-smeared lips as they ate, filled with joy at the morning's lifesaving gifts. When they had finished, Kirima buried the remaining meat under a corner of the bearskin floor of the shelter, near Cloud Man's feet.

Then the glint of a sparkling object among Kirima's equipment attracted Cikuq's attention. The older boy pointed. "What bright thing is that?"

Revived, the ache in his belly calmed, Kirima jumped up and held out Cloud Man's tubular piece of ice. "It came with Cloud Man. He treasures it, but I have not seen such a thing before," the boy said, hefting the object in his hand. "It is hollow like the leg bone of a caribou."

"I can see through it," Cikuq said, taking the object and holding it up to his face. "It is as cold and hard as the sea ice that supports the white bear in winter. What is it made of?"

"I do not know. It is a strange color, too, like an old walrus at molting time." Kirima took the object from his friend. "I can see your face through it, too, but it looks distorted, like your reflection does in rippling water. And, even stranger, this tube of ice does not melt with the heat of my breath, see?"

Kirima blew on the object, and his breath wrapped the object in a fog that slowly dissipated as he watched. "Did you see that?"
Cikuq took the hard piece of ice and blew on it as well. "This is like magic."

With a chuff, Red Dog wriggled out of Cloud Man's embrace and trotted over to Kirima's sled, sniffing the strange object in Cikuq's hand. Seeing this, Gray Dog whined and pulled at his tether, his feet making scraping sounds as he scratched through the snow. Kirima untied him, and Gray Dog dragged the boy over to the sled, shouldering Red Dog out of the way. He danced around the boy, trying to get closer to the curious object.

The brownish residue at the bottom of the object caught Cikuq's eye. He pointed. "What is that?"

Gray Dog punched Cikuq's hand with his nose, whining.

"Do you want to smell?" Cikuq held the tube out.

Gray Dog took a sniff and jumped back, sneezing violently and shaking his head.

Kirima smiled at that, and taking the tube from Cikuq, he put it up to his own nose. He jerked back and wrinkled his face at the pungent scent. "Phew!" he exclaimed. "I do not wonder that Cloud Man was sick. This smells like a bag of summer berries forgotten at the bottom of the women's gathering basket."

He handed the tube to his companion, but Cikuq waved his hand. "I believe you," he said with a grimace.

Kirima thumped the tube against his leg, testing its strength and solidity. Gray Dog leaped upward, trying to grab the ice tube. Kirima pirouetted, turning in a circle to keep the dog from grabbing the object. "Back, big dog, or I'll tie you up again," he said sharply, holding the tube above Gray Dog's head. "I would like to take this strange thing back to the seal camp and see if Angakok can explain it."

When Gray Dog saw the tube disappear into Kirima's front pocket, he jumped toward Cloud Man, nose twitching. Before the dog could get himself in trouble, Kirima grabbed him by his collar and led him slowly up to Cloud Man, who lay on his back, neck extended and lips parted. Then Kirima gestured to Red Dog, who lay down obediently next to the sleeping stranger once again, yawning and putting her head on her paws. Her demeanor had a calming effect on the gray one, and he threw himself down next to her, black nostrils quivering as he sniffed across her body to catch Cloud Man's strange scent. Kirima tucked the smaller of the two seal bladders next to Gray Dog, and the two dogs watched Kirima from under their dark eyebrow dots, eyes shifting back and forth as Kirima moved about the camp.

"See this in my sled bag? There is another curious thing that belongs to Cloud Man." Kirima pulled the cold, gray stick from his equipment pile.

"See how heavy this stick is! What do you think it does?"

Cikuq examined the article, tapping down the length of it and testing its strength. Then he shook his head. "Only Cloud Man and the gods know. It does not bend, and one end is hollow, like the flight bones of an *ookpik.*"

"No, the stick is much larger than a snowy owl," Kirima countered. "Perhaps Cloud Man will show us its purpose when he wakes."

Kirima replaced the stick in his sled bag. Then, content to wait for Cloud Man to awaken, Kirima picked up the larger of the two seal bladders and turned it inside out. "Perhaps this stranger will be grateful we saved his life," he said, beginning to scrub the lining of the bladder clean with handfuls of snow. "He may then reward us for saving him from the spirit world."

"Yes, he may use his power to help the People."

Kirima laughed as he turned the bladder back. "But what power does he have now?" he asked as he packed the bladder with snow. "He is one step from the spirit world and had not the sense to keep himself safe alone on the ice."

Cloud Man grunted suddenly and turned over. Startled, both dogs raised their heads to look at him, then jumped up and leaped away, digging two new nests in the snow a few feet from the boys.

Cloud Man slowly sat up and looked about, beginning to shake with cold. His teeth chattered loudly, and his lips turned the color of the river rock at the summer camp. Kirima put his hands behind the stranger, supporting him. He blew warm breath into the neck of Cloud Man's parka and rubbed his chest vigorously to warm the white skin. Slowly, Cloud Man's trembling abated and his breathing calmed.

"Red Dog," Kirima called, struggling to his feet as he laid the Kabloona back down. The boy grabbed Red Dog's collar and tugged her toward Cloud Man. The red one resisted at first; then, tongue lolling, she settled next to the strange-smelling man.

"Keep Cloud Man warm again while I bring him water," Kirima told her.

Kirima covered both the dog and the stranger with the bearskin. "He will return to the path to the Sky Village if he cannot drink and begins to shiver again," he told Cikuq. Then, turning, he made a fierce face at the gray one. "And Gray Dog, stay away from the meat!"

Kirima picked up the bladder that had rested against Gray Dog's side. He shook it, and, satisfied that the water inside had not frozen, he poured a few drops slowly down Cloud Man's throat. The stranger coughed, then swallowed. He took another sip and opened his eyes. Then he drank deeply. Cloud Man sat for a few minutes as strength returned to his sick body.

"Tell me about this strange man," Cikuq said, breaking the silence. "How does he come to be with us, here, at our camp?"

Pleased to share the tale, Kirima described his journey to the giant *umiaks*. Cikuq sat quietly, listening while Kirima related in detail all that transpired between the Cloud Men on the great *kayak*. Kirima glanced at the Kabloona; then, wishing to include him, began to pantomime Cloud Man being hit on the head and shoved off the boat. He went to his sled bag and picked up the tubular ice.

Cloud Man nodded, following the gestures. Then he began mumbling sentence after sentence, stringing together an incomprehensible chain of guttural words in an up-and-down cadence of harsh sounds. A hint of anger painted his words. Kirima put a placating hand on Cloud Man's shoulder, remembering the ferocity of the attack by his *umiak* brother. Perhaps all Kabloonas were that violent.

"This man has been cold and asleep for a long time," Cikuq said. "He must be hungry now. We should see if he can eat. It will help warm him and keep him on this side of the spirit world."

"My own stomach tells me it is time for us to eat again," Kirima said.

Uncovering the food cache, Kirima divided the lemming meat into three portions, and Cikuq offered the stranger a bit of the lemming. Cloud Man took it into his mouth with a grimace, but as he began to chew, his face relaxed into a smile.

"Ah, Cloud Man is looking stronger and stronger," Kirima said, biting into his portion.

"Ah, good, and I see the color of sunrise has come back to his face," said Cikuq as he licked lemming fat from his fingers. "He no longer shivers with the cold, and he can sit up without your help."

The boys continued to talk as they ate. A short while later, Cloud Man rose on one knee and looked around the shelter. Both boys fell silent as the stranger stood shakily. Then, speaking to Kirima, the Kabloona held out his hand, palm upward. Puzzled, the boy looked first at the stranger's hand, then at his face. When the boy did not respond, the man hauled back the fur bedding, uncovering the snow underneath. His voice grew loud, and he turned toward Kirima's sled with a faltering although purposeful step.

Kirima jumped up, ready to flee. He turned to Cikuq. "Anger claims the spirit of this man. Who are these people who are maddened so readily and show their emotions like children?"

Cloud Man searched the equipment pile, and with a cry, he seized the long, gray stick. He sat back down near Kirima and inspected the stick carefully, manipulating the pieces affixed to its sides. *Click, snick, clack.* Then he checked the pockets of his parka and pulled out a handful of shiny pebbles, pointed on one end, blunt on the other. They glinted and gleamed, reflecting the morning light, rattling against each other with a clinking sound unlike any Kirima had heard before. Finally, Cloud Man gave a quick nod and returned the pebbles to his pocket. His face relaxed. He packed the stick back inside the sled.

I wonder what this stick is that concerns Cloud Man so. Kirima frowned. *What is its use? And what are the pebbles that seem to go with the stick?*

Cikuq pointed to the piece of tubular ice. "If this Kabloona is as angry as he seems, he probably wants the ice tube back as well."

Kirima took the hollow cylinder from his pocket and offered it to Cloud Man. The stranger made a throaty sound, not unlike the grunt Gray Dog gave just before being fed, and grabbed the object from the boy. Then Cloud Man nodded and held up one finger, then pointed to the tube. He scooped some snow up from the ground and painstakingly poked it into the cavity of the tube. He did this again and again until the cavity was partially filled with snow. Then he put the tube inside his coat. When he brought it out, the snow had melted. He tipped the tube to his mouth and took a sip.

Kirima turned to Cikuq, puzzled. "What great work for a sip of water. Do these people not have large seal bladders and soapstone lamps for melting snow?"

Greatly recovered, Cloud Man smacked his lips and handed the tube to Kirima. He gestured to the Inuuk to take the ice cylinder, pointing from his chest to Kirima's.

Kirima nodded in delight. *Why, it is a gift!*

Pointing to the tube, Cloud Man uttered an unfamiliar word. The boy attempted to imitate the strange new sound.

"Bod-dul," Kirima said, smiling. "Bod-dul."

"Bod-dul," Cikuq repeated, pointing to the tube.

Cloud Man nodded vigorously and laughed. He walked slowly round the ice shelf, squinting at the setting sun and looking in the direction of the ocean. He pointed, then put his hand on his chest, and pointed again out to sea. He gestured in this manner several times.

A thrill of excitement raced up Kirima's spine. "I think Cloud Man wants to return to his *umiak*!"

"Yes!" said Cikuq. "You saved the stranger's life! Now the stranger will repay in kind. He can help paddle the *umiak* back to his native lands and clear the way for the seals. He can save the lives of the People."

"Let us camp here and leave in the morning," Kirima said. "If we take Cloud Man back in the dark, the strangers on the *umiak* may not see that we come in peace."

Early the next morning, Kirima arose and scanned the landscape, looking for signs of oncoming inclement weather. Clouds were gathering on the far horizon, dark and ominous. With great effort, he shook Cikuq awake.

"We must hasten before another storm pins us inside our sled cave again."

Their activity woke Cloud Man, who crawled out of the shelter and watched as the boys gathered up the last of the lemming meat for the dogs.

Kirima nudged Gray Dog with his toe to wake him. "Lazy dog," he said with affection, offering the gray one some of the meat. "You sleep as soundly as Cikuq!"

When the last bits of lemming had vanished down the dog's throats, Kirima and Cikuq began setting their sleds to rights and hitching the dogs to their gang lines. Red Dog went willingly to her place, but her gray companion had other ideas. Cloud Man stepped back, holding his hands toward the dog as Gray Dog skittered toward him, tail waving slightly above his back with nervous tension. The gray one danced closer, laying his ears back. Then he gave Cloud Man a submissive grin, pulling only the front of his lips up without wrinkling his muzzle. His tail wagged sideways in greeting.

Kirima caught the dog deftly by his harness and led him to the sled.

"Gray Dog just wants to say hello to a strange man and his clothes," Cikuq said to Cloud Man.

"Sled dogs are friendly dogs," Kirima said over his shoulder. "They learn with their noses about everyone they meet." He kneeled by the gray one, putting his arms around the dog's neck and giving him a hug. Gray Dog wriggled in pleasure, his tail wagging furiously.

Then Gray Dog danced away from Kirima and punched Red Dog in the shoulder with his nose. Red Dog snapped at him and held her tail high. She put a paw over his back and growled a warning. Gray Dog lowered his head and put his ears back in submission. He curled his tail between his legs. Red Dog put her chin over his back, then nosed him playfully on the shoulder.

"She forgives you, Gray Dog," Kirima said. "Line out."

The gray one wagged his tail and took his place in front of the sled as Kirima motioned for Cloud Man to climb into the sled basket. His own team already poised to run, Cikuq waited as Kirima packed his gear around the stranger and covered him with the bearskin. Then, shouting to their teams, the two Inuit headed back across the tumbled shore ice toward the sea. Cloud Man whooped, too, and raised his hands in the air, clasping his hands together and shaking them up and down. Kirima did not look back, but the panting of Cikuq's dogs and the creak of his companion's sled were audible close behind.

Just before mid-morning, the boys reached the shore. A dark lump caught Kirima's eye.

"Seal!" he shouted, gesturing to his quest partner.

"Seal!" Cikuq echoed. "Seal!"

The ringed seal's dark fur set it off against the white background. It had hauled itself out on a sheet of ice beside its breathing hole. Beyond the seal lay the dark shapes of many more seals resting on the ice.

"Cloud Man has lifted the curse of the *umiak*!" Kirima rejoiced. "The seals have returned!"

"Let us move away from these many seals lest we frighten them off," Cikuq shouted. "Turn, dogs, turn!"

Kirima and Cikuq turned around, putting the distance of many sled lengths between themselves and the seals. The younger boy backed the sled onto itself to slow the dogs, grabbed Red Dog's tug line, and set his snow hook deeply into the icy surface. Despite his impatience to hunt the seal, he made yellow water over the hook, freezing it securely into the ice shelf, then took the time to double-check its strength.

"I see Cloud Man is beginning to shiver again," Kirima said to Cikuq. "One of us may have to keep him warm while the other hunts the seal."

Cikuq yawned. "We will take turns," he said. "I will hunt when you have returned. Until then, I will stay with Cloud Man and wrap both of us up in the bearskin and take a nap."

When the two men were settled, and Cloud Man's shivering abated, Kirima reached into the sled bag. A cry of distress rose into Kirima's throat; he had forgotten that his sealing spear was gone. Chewing the inside of his cheek in irritation, he grabbed his long spear and snow knife instead. He paused. *How will I proceed?*

"I will take my long spear," he told Cikuq to cover up his chagrin. "I can reach the seal from a greater distance and not cause the rest of the seals to panic and flee into the ocean."

Cikuq nodded sleepily. "Wake me when you come back."

Kirima walked to within sight of the seals, then got on his hands and knees, creeping stealthily across the ice shelf. He held his *pana* between his teeth and slid his whaling harpoon beside him as quietly as he could. Closer and closer he crawled. He ducked behind the uplifted ice ridge and crept closer still, barely breathing.

Quietly, quietly, he thought.

Just as Kirima was within range, the seal twitched and raised its head, looking about for danger. Kirima froze and held his breath. A seal's eyesight was keen underwater, but on land, the seal had difficulty distinguishing between a man lying prone on the ice and another sleeping seal. Slowly, the seal laid its head back on the ice. Finally, it closed its eyes.

Kirima held still, slowly moving his hands under his chest. Then the boy gathered his legs under himself, readying his harpoon. Suddenly, the seal jerked its head up, startled. Before Kirima could launch his weapon, it threw itself back down its breathing hole into the sea.

Warroar! Rrrroah! Warroar!

The roar was loud! The roar was close!

Nanuq! The white bear! Nanuq was upon him!

Chapter 11

The white bear bellowed again and stood up to its full height. It bared its teeth and snarled, curling its muzzle in menace.

Kirima's heart almost burst with shock. *Eee-yi!* Nanuq! Nanuq!

And the ear! The ear!

This was his mortal enemy, the bear that sent Qannik to the spirit world! The bear that claimed the life of his father! The bear was here!

Kirima's heart contracted in panic, his eyes opened wide, and a small cry sprang from his lips.

"*The bear! The bear!*"

Screeeee, scrape! went the bear's claws on the crusted surface as it dropped to the ground.

Screeeee, scrape!

Kirima stood frozen with fear, watching the bear approach. The great beast lumbered around the ice ridge and lowered its mighty head, swinging it back and forth. It gnashed its teeth and bellowed.

The need to stay alive gave the boy sudden courage, and he reacted by instinct alone.

"No!" Kirima shouted, stepping toward the bear. Still clutching his spear and *pana,* he waved his arms in the air. "You took my father! You will *not* take me!"

Holding his long spear out to keep the bear at a distance, he threw his snow knife with all his might at the bear's huge head, aiming for its eyes.

The *pana* missed its mark and bounced off the white bear's skull, nicking the skin and landing harmlessly on the ice.

The bear roared again and advanced toward Kirima. A trickle of blood ran down the side of its face. It reared up again and struck out with one of its great paws. Only one sled length separated the two. The bear halted its forward motion, swinging its head back and forth.

Quickly, Kirima held up his whaling harpoon; the shaft of the long spear trembled in his hand. He gritted his teeth and set the butt end of his spear firmly into the snowy ground, just as his own father surely had. He angled the point toward the great, white bulk of the roaring bear.

O Father, my father, send me strength! Send me the courage that failed you so long ago.

The boy recoiled as the rancid odor of the bear's foul breath blew toward him in the slight breeze. He gripped his spear, his entire body shaking, as the bear slowly advanced. The ice creaked under its great weight. One step, then two.

The bear lifted its head, revealing the scarred and ugly stump of its left ear.

Legs threatening to buckle, but heart filled with unexpected courage, Kirima stood his ground.

The bear loomed over the boy as it rose on its hind legs. Its mighty roar reverberated deep in Kirima's chest. He tensed, gasping for breath, spear pointing upward toward the menace advancing upon him.

BE BRAVE! YOU ARE NOT YOUR FATHER!

Kirima's head fought with his heart.

Do not move! Do not show fear! Brace the spear, do not move!

The bear lunged another step forward, claws extended. Its mouth opened wide as its roar thundered across the ice shelf.

Kirima threw his weight against the spear to anchor it, summoning all his courage as he braced himself in the bear's path.

Run! Run away fast! shouted his heart. But his head whispered, *Stand strong, stay, stay, brace yourself, stand strong.*

The bear loomed over the boy. Its teeth glinted in the spring light. Webs of drool hung from the bear's upper lip. The bear gathered itself to spring. Its jaws dripped saliva. Its eyes glittered with fury.

"Come get me!" Kirima screamed. His blood pounded through his body. His fear suddenly vanished. Only anger remained, followed by a deadly calm in the very center of his being.

The bear roared a roar that even the moon goddess could hear. Kirima braced himself against the spear.

The bear lunged. Down toward the young man came the bear. The spear tip pierced the bear's hide.

Crunch!

The bear's weight drove the sharp tip of the harpoon deep into its chest. Kirima jumped backward, avoiding the bear's falling body.

With a sharp *crack!* the shaft of the spear splintered in two.

Crash! The ice cracked as the bear fell to the ground before the young man.

The bear was up in an instant, blood gushing from its wound. With a howl of pain, it leaped forward. Its great paw lashed out, slicing Kirima's leggings as its claws gashed the young man's thigh.

The force of the bear's attack knocked Kirima backwards. Reeling, he fell hard onto the ice. He kicked himself away from the bear, but his feet were unable to gain purchase on the slippery surface.

The bear roached its back, gathering its legs under itself, preparing for the kill.

The sound of howling dogs in the distance floated into Kirima's consciousness.

Then a Boom, louder than the crack that follows lightning, deafened the young man.

The bear smashed backwards onto the ice, blood pumping from its head. This time its body lay still.

Deafened, Kirima shook his head. The ringing in the young man's ears muted the yelping of the sled dogs behind him. Kirima looked at the bear. He looked at the harpoon shaft protruding from the white fur of the bear's chest. He looked at the hole in the bear's skull.

Kirima turned. A smoky, acrid scent, wholly new to the young man, reached his nostrils.

Cloud Man appeared in the distance, more than ten sled lengths away, moving steadily across the ice toward the young man, Cikuq a short distance behind. The stranger carried his heavy stick, one end of which smoked gray vapor into the cold air. He was laughing heartily as he waved his free hand in the air, but Kirima could hear only a faint sound coming from Cloud Man's open mouth.

Kirima shook his head again to dispel the ringing in his ears. Cloud Man crunched up to him and leaned down, slapping Kirima on the back.

Kirima stared at the Kabloona in confusion and awe. Did the sound of thunder come from Cloud Man's stick? Did it make that hole in Nanuq's head?

Slowly Kirima's hearing returned. He was aware of the sound of his own breath coming in short gasps. He listened to his dogs shrieking in the distance. He heard the slap of seawater on the side of the seal's escape route. He heard the rasp of his quest companion's boots on the ice as Cikuq hurried to join Cloud Man.

Without rising, Kirima reached a trembling hand toward the thunderstick. Cloud Man lowered the weapon so the young man could touch its gray shaft. The same acrid scent wafted from the eye in one end of the weapon. As the heat of its power seeped through his thick gloves, the young man's hand recoiled from its fiery surface.

Cikuq reached out to contact the cooling shaft as well, his eyes wide in amazement. He and Kirima exchanged looks of incredulity. Then Cikuq stepped over to the bear, and, putting his hands on his hips, looked down at the beast.

Kirima twisted around to speak to his quest companion. "This weapon killed Nanuq, yet Cloud Man was a great distance away." The pain in his thigh made him gasp. "How can this be?"

"The shaman was correct," Cikuq murmured, reaching out with one foot to touch the wound in the bear's skull. "Holes the size of a ptarmigan's eggs."

Still sprawled on the ice, Kirima gaped at the fallen bear. The great beast lay on its side, blood swiftly congealing around its head. Long, black claws protruded from feet the size of the drum at a drum dance. Its fur was yellowed with age, its teeth as long as Kirima's middle fingers.

Turning to the Kabloona, Kirima pointed to the thunderstick and then behind him at the bear. His hand shook in the pale sunlight, and the young man hastily hid it in the pocket of his parka.

The Kabloona nodded vigorously, grinning, and held the stick up to his shoulder, sighting down the shaft. "Boom!" Cloud Man yelled, suddenly pulling up on the stick to point it skyward. He gestured toward the bear, his hands pantomiming the bear falling. A toothy grin split his pale face.

"What a weapon!" Kirima said in awe, pain forgotten. He twisted around to contemplate the fallen white hulk once again.

Why, this bear is only a bear, as mortal as I am, and we both live with the goddesses' blessings. I did not run when Nanuq charged. I held my spear steady.

Elation and triumph swelled in his chest. *I have vanquished my foe, and I have conquered my enemy! No longer will I live with the shame of my father's cowardice.*

His fear of all bears slid away as sinuously as a seal slips down into her breathing hole. Now the spirits of the seals and whales would return to the land of the Netsilik. His people would not starve. He and Cikuq had saved Cloud Man from the spirit world. The quest was fulfilled.

Kirima started to get up, wanting to pace off the length of the fallen bear, but stumbled as the pain in his leg penetrated his consciousness once more. He examined his thigh through the hole in his trousers. Crouching, Cikuq used the torn hide of Kirima's trousers to bind the wound as best he could. Nodding thanks, Kirima flexed his knee, grimacing.

"I think I can walk without it bleeding too badly." Kirima stood, and although his leg was very sore, he found he could function.

Following Cikuq's lead, Cloud Man helped turn Nanuq over on its side, wrenching the harpoon from its chest. Kirima retrieved his *pana* and stared down at the bear. "Enough skins for more than four pairs of men's trousers," Kirima murmured. "Enough meat for a village drum dance...."

The task of skinning and butchering with only his snow knife would be arduous; Cikuq was already carving a line around one of the bear's hind legs, popping the wrist joint backwards in order to pare the hide away from the foot. Kirima knelt on the opposite side, grasping the other leg, prepared to do his share of skinning. But Kirima's snow knife was too long and dull to pierce the hide of the bear.

"This is not possible," Kirima said, looking at Cikuq in dismay. He held up his *pana*. "A snow knife cannot do the job of a skinning knife. I cannot cut into the bear."

"I will do it," Cikuq said, but as he rose to change places with Kirima, Cloud Man grunted and waved his hand to halt the young men's progress.

Cloud Man laid his thunderstick down and withdrew a knife from the front pocket of his parka. Its blade glinted, flashing sunlight across the faces of the quest companions. The sight transfixed Kirima. He blinked, admiring the blade, the walrus tusk handle. Here was a knife!

Crouching beside the younger of the two men, Cloud Man plunged the blade into the section Kirima had abandoned. Astounded, Kirima watched as the knife cut effortlessly through the bear's skin, fascia, and muscle to release the hide from the hind leg.

Kirima's mouth gaped. *Another weapon of the Cloud Men! How have they come by such things?*

Looking at the Inuit hunters, Cloud Man raised his pale eyebrows in question as he gestured over the bear's hide with his knife. Cikuq indicated the necessary cuts to slice through the bear's skin. Meanwhile, Kirima used his *pana* to separate the skin from the flesh underneath, pulling back the hide and sliding his snow knife between it and the fascia below. All the while, he marveled at the heaviness of Nanuq's head, the size of its paws, and the thickness of its fur.

What a magnificent creature!

The morning turned into day as the men carefully finished skinning the bear. Cikuq motioned to Cloud Man, pointing to his knife. When the Kabloona handed it over, the young man cut into the bear's abdomen, exposing the innards.

"The honor is yours," Cikuq said, handing Kirima the stranger's knife. "It is your courage that halted the bear's progress and made it possible for

Cloud Man to use his weapon to kill the bear."

Kirima took the knife and held it over the bear's body cavity, which steamed in the spring air. Carefully, he removed the bear's liver, setting it reverently on the ice.

"Bear liver is poison," Kirima said to Cloud Man. "The People do not eat it. They offer it to the sea to honor Nanuq's spirit."

Cloud Man nodded as if he understood.

Kirima wiped his bloodied hands on the snow and touched the bear claw amulet sewn into the neck of his parka. He then lifted the liver and carried it, wet and heavy in his hands, to the seal's breathing hole. He held the offering over the water, the element with which the bear was most at home; then, he sang a tribute to the great spirit of the white bear who had given its life that day:

> *Great White Bear*
> *Great Bear of the North*
> *Run with the spirits*
> *Of all bears before*
> *Run in peace*
> *Run in joy*
> *Join the Great Ones*
> *Dance in the sky*

He opened his hands, and with a gentle splash, the liver dropped into the water and disappeared into its black depths.

Kirima turned to Cikuq. "This man and his traveling companion will take Cloud Man back to his *umiak* so the Cloud People can leave this land. And then you and I will return home to the seal camp."

Cikuq nodded in agreement.

"And the bear? How shall we divide it?" Kirima asked.

Cikuq gestured to the carcass. "This is a big bear. You and I will share the skin equally. We will keep enough meat for our journey home and for our families to feast when we return. Cloud Man will keep a like portion, because he killed the bear with his thunderstick."

Kirima smiled. "We three men are now Nanuq partners, sharing equally."

Chapter 12

As the afternoon sun slipped toward the sea, Kirima, Cikuq, and Cloud Man worked together to finish butchering the bear and complete the task while enough light remained to make the journey back to the *umiak*. Kirima worked behind Cloud Man's cuts, laboriously sawing through the bear's flesh with his snow knife.

"This sharp knife cuts through meat and bone with such ease!" Kirima said, gesturing numerous times to the flashing blade in Cloud Man's hand. "I cannot imagine what kind of river rock would give it such a cutting edge!"

The Kabloona smiled and handed the young man the knife, handle first. Kirima took it and marveled anew as he sliced effortlessly through the flesh of the bear.

When they were through, Kirima and Cikuq walked back to the camp and brought the dogs and their sleds to the place that the bear fell. The dogs pulled hard on their harnesses, testing the patience of the Inuit men as they staked the dogs out near the butchering site.

Returning to the carcass, Kirima cut a small portion of bear meat, dividing it in three. The men ate ravenously. Licking his lips, Cloud Man reached out his knife for another piece of bear meat, but Kirima stopped him.

"Too much food on a stomach grown small from starvation will make one sick," he said, shaking his hand over the pile of meat. "You have been without food for too long." He pointed to Cloud Man's stomach and grimaced, shaking his head back and forth.

"Ahhh..." said Cloud Man with understanding, wiping the knife on the snow and slipping it into the waistband of his trousers.

Cikuq divided the bearskin in equal portions and showed the Kabloona how to wrap the meat in the skins. Frantic to smell the parcels of meat, both dogs yapped and leaped against their restraining tethers, but as Kirima bundled the hide and meat into the sleds, Cloud Man grabbed Red Dog and Cikuq caught Gray Dog. Both men held the dogs fast while Kirima finished loading the sled. He smiled to see Cloud Man ruffle the fur on Red Dog's neck and chest.

With the sleds loaded and creaking under their sudden burdens, Cikuq clipped an extra line of caribou sinew to his sled and tied it about his waist, fan hitching his dogs and himself to his sled. Looking down at his bandaged leg, Kirima furrowed his brow. Six—two men and four dogs—were needed to pull the sleds' heavy burdens.

Then Cloud Man tapped Cikuq on the shoulder. He gestured first to the sinew lines, then to himself. The young man smiled and found another line for Cloud Man, hitching him to Kirima's sled.

"Kirima," Cikuq said, turning to his quest partner as he lined out his team. "You will walk alongside us without pulling, so the wound on your leg will not start to bleed again." "I see the wisdom in your words," Kirima said. "I will keep the dogs in line."

Then he held up his hand, indicating that his companions wait a moment. "Today we three became Nanuq brothers, one life saving the other. We honored the spirit of the great bear. Cikuq and I saved Cloud Man's life, and he, in turn, repaid us by appealing to the sea goddess. Now she will send seals to our people."

He checked the line around Cloud Man's shoulders and adjusted the fit. The Kabloona grinned, patting the traces around his upper body and nodding.

Pulling in tandem with the sled dogs, Cikuq and Cloud Man trudged off—one man tall and strong again, the other standing tall as well. Alongside walked the third, although moving with a decided limp. The ease with which the stranger fell into Cikuq's rhythm surprised the Inuit men.

Soon they came upon the ice-locked *umiak* sitting quietly, its tall antlers pointing toward the sky. The white hides attached to the antlers billowed in the breeze, slowly drying as the last rime of frost thawed and dripped onto the deck. The other boat lay on its side, antlers touching the ground, almost completely crushed by the sea ice. There was no sign of people on board either vessel.

With wide eyes and gaping mouth, Cikuq stopped short, abruptly bringing his dogs to a halt.

Kirima turned to Cikuq. "The nearest *umiak* is still locked in the embrace of the sea," he said. "The second *umiak* is past repair."

"Never could I have imagined such a giant boat!" Cikuq continued to gawk, dogs and sled forgotten, and slowly shook his head.

With a small smile, Kirima motioned to his friend to continue on. Cikuq and Cloud Man helped their dogs drag the sleds to the side of the *umiak,* and the men dropped the sled's traces. Kirima, still limping, quickly caught the dogs and held them fast.

Cupping his hands around his mouth, Cloud Man called out. Soon one of his fellow seafarers appeared on the floor of the *umiak*. Shock showed clearly on the other Kabloona's face; he began to shout, gesturing toward the men below. Several more men appeared, and their strange language floated into the air as they conversed, pointing downward.

I hope Cloud Man is boasting about my bravery as the bear charged and how I, Kirima, withstood the bear's attack, the young man thought as Cloud Man talked and gesticulated to his ship board companions.

The bluejackets lowered a rope ladder, followed by a large basket made from a dark substance unlike any Kirima had seen before. The material looked like walrus hide, but the *clunk* as it bumped against the hull was not unlike the sound of driftwood tossed against the rocks on the seashore.

Cloud Man turned to his new Inuit friends and bowed. He picked up the thunderstick from the sled bag and held it out to Kirima.

The Inuuk stood, irresolute. *Does Cloud Man intend to give me his fearsome weapon?*

Gently, Cloud Man shoved the stick into Kirima's chest, and nodded emphatically when the Inuit grasped the cold, gray shaft.

Kirima snatched his hands back and shook his head. *Such a frightening and magical harpoon has no place in the peaceful life of the Inuit!* He stepped back, fluttering his hands back and forth to indicate refusal.

The magic of this weapon is too strong; it might anger the spirits and bring misfortune back to the People. I will ask for the knife instead.

Kirima gestured toward Cloud Man's jacket. His new friend shrugged, removing the blue parka and handing it to the young Inuit.

Kirima laughed and shook his head. "Cikuq, do you have need of a parka that will not keep you warm in a sudden cold snap?"

Cikuq chuckled, and Cloud Man looked perplexed at their mirth.

Kirima returned the parka and pointed to the knife held in the waistband of Cloud Man's trousers. The Kabloona shrugged and shook his head, clearly bewildered, as he handed the knife to Kirima.

Kirima bowed low in thanks, smiling up into Cloud Man's eyes. Then he stood, hefting the knife in his hands, his eyes glinting with appreciation.

"Sharp, well balanced, a knife from another world," he said.

Cikuq added, "A knife worthy of the bravest of hunters."

Kirima tried to suppress the pride that overcame him at these words, but his face turned pink with pleasure. To hide his reaction, he fetched Cloud Man's portion of the bear meat and handed the parcel to his new friend.

Cloud Man grinned and placed his bear meat on the ground. Then he grasped Kirima's hand in his. He gave it a squeeze and a mighty shake and turned back toward his *umiak*. With a small sigh of regret, Kirima watched Cloud Man prepare to leave them. He loaded his portion of the bear meat into the basket and tugged on its long line, making certain the basket was secure.

A freshening wind brought the scent of spring, a promise of warmth to Kirima's face. Though he knew Cloud Man would not understand, Kirima spoke anyway. "Soon the sea goddess will release your *umiak* from the winter sea. Perhaps the spirit of another time will bring back my Nanuq brother to hunt with me again."

Cloud Man touched Kirima's shoulder, giving it a squeeze.

With a creaking sound, the basket was hoisted up to the deck. Cloud Man gestured for Kirima to wait, then leaped onto the rope ladder. He clambered up to the floor of the *umiak,* then ducked inside the boat's wooden house. He quickly reappeared and, with a mighty heave and a broad smile, threw a square object down to the Inuuk. With a clank and a bounce, it landed at Kirima's feet.

Kirima picked up the container, which was made of a hard, gray material he had never seen before. Smooth and solid under his fingers, its construction was neat and precise. The top flashed and glinted as the pale spring sunshine reflected the light back toward Kirima's eyes. The box rattled slightly when he shook it; he held it up to his nose, but he could not discern the box's contents.

Kirima handed the box to Cikuq, who also examined it closely.

"This is a well-constructed container!" Cikuq said. "The lid is very tight; I cannot open it."

Kirima struggled with the lid for a few seconds. "I cannot open it, either," he said. Shrugging, he tucked it in his sled bad. Then he turned and raised his hand in thanks to Cloud Man.

Cloud Man raised his hand in return. Then, as Kirima and Cikuq continued to watch the action aboard the great *kayak*, Cloud Man turned away to busy himself on the boat.

The bluejackets climbed up the *umiak's* tall antlers and laboriously furled the white skins ballooning in the breeze. Cloud Man assisted from below, pulling on lines and making them fast onto large pieces of antler fastened to the sides of the boat. The skins billowed in protest as the men aloft fought to bring them under control. All the while, Cloud Man talked to his *umiak* brothers, stopping occasionally to explain his words with gestures.

Kirima watched with fascination. "These men cooperate on the *umiak* like our people cooperate during the caribou hunt," he told Cikuq. "And yet they fight with each other and abandon one of their kind on the ice."

"They are indeed complicated and beyond understanding," Cikuq said, shrugging.

When the skins were folded and the spars were all but naked, the men disappeared into the large snow house on top of the deck; only Cloud Man lingered behind. He held his hand up in farewell, and Kirima and Cikuq returned the wave. Then Cloud Man followed his companions into the large *iglu*, and the giant *kayak* again looked deserted as it awaited the thaw.

Once again aware of the aching in his leg, Kirima turned his attention to his wound. He undressed and carefully cleaned the deep cuts with snow, then covered the wound with a length of fox skin to keep out the cold. With his shiny, new *pilaut*, he deftly cut a length of caribou skin from his trousers and rebound his thigh with it.

Cikuq helped Kirima onto the foot planks at the back of his sled. Then the older hunter took his place behind his own sled. Kirima circled his dogs, and the two young men turned south. Kirima looked back again and again at the great *umiaks* until the boats were but specks on the horizon.

Eventually, both men stopped the dogs and gave them snacks from their small caches of bear meat. Kirima's injury was quite painful, hot and throbbing; his wounded leg had been tested to its limits, compensating for flexing and bouncing of his sled. He climbed down from the sled platform and gently rubbed a handful of snow on the wound, gratified to see that it looked clean and dry.

"The box," Cikuq said as he helped Kirima bandage his thigh. "What is inside?"

The box! His wound forgotten, Kirima withdrew the container from his sled bag and used his new knife to pry open the lid. Inside he found many more small boxes, lined up neatly, all identical, cold and smooth as river rock. Were these made from the same substance that gave his new knife such color and sheen?

He struggled unsuccessfully to open one of the small boxes, then took his new *pilaut* and stabbed a hole in the top. Much to his surprise, Kirima was rewarded with the rich aroma of meat.

"It is meat in a stone box! How do the Cloud Men manage to do this?"

With a whine and a bark, Kirima's dogs turned back on their traces in search of the tantalizing scent. Cikuq's team jumped toward the odor also, tangling themselves in their own traces.

"Whoa!" Cikuq cried as he stomped his snow hook into the crust, securing his sled.

"You bad wolf!" Kirima scolded Gray Dog, untangling the tug lines from Red Dog's legs. The red one lunged toward the sled, snuffling for the source of the aroma, and Kirima scolded her, too. Seeing his companion's difficulty in lining out his dogs, Cikuq abandoned his own team and went to the aid of his friend.

"I thank the man who has come to my aid once again," Kirima said. Cikuq nodded, giving his companion a hearty grin.

When order was restored and both teams were once again pointing homeward, Kirima returned the gray box to his sled bag. Then he stowed the knife carefully beneath the sled's bearskin, where Cloud Man's bod-dul also lay safely nestled. He smiled as he pictured bringing these gifts back to the village. The tube of ice he would give to Grandmother. She would put it to good use and have a wonderful time sharing it with others in the village. And how amazed Apak's face would be when Kirima brought the knife back to his grandfather! What would he think about such a gift?

"Kirima, you do not need to drive your dogs," Cikuq said, interrupting his companion's thoughts. "Ride instead; your dogs will follow my team home."

Kirima nodded. "I see the wisdom of your suggestion," he said, gingerly rubbing his injured thigh and smiling gratefully.

He covered himself with the bearskin, getting comfortable. Now was the time for rest, for healing. This was traveling weather, and with Red Dog leading the way, his dogs would follow Cikuq's team home as they traveled by the light of the stars.

As the two teams drew farther and farther from the sea, Kirima found he was too excited to sleep. His mind was busy telling and retelling the story of the journey, the *umiak*, and, most importantly, the killing of the great bear. He would tell of the white bear's sudden appearance, of his notched ear stump. He remembered the feel of the bear's claws as they penetrated the muscle of his thigh. He memorized the precise setting of his spear, his own bravery standing his ground as the bear charged. He pictured the spear driving deeply into the bear's chest and heard once again the crack of the broken shaft.

"Boom!" Kirima shouted, imitating the fierce cry of the thunderstick. "Boom! Boom!"

His two dogs paused in mid-stride, and turned their heads toward the sled. Kirima laughed aloud at their reaction. Glancing at each other in accord, the dogs turned back toward the trail and continued on their way, leaning into their harnesses.

"Boom!" Kirima yelled again. "Boom!" He held his arms in the air, imitating Cloud Man. He pretended to slap himself on the back.

He heard Cikuq's laughter from the short distance ahead. "Boom!" Cikuq yelled.

Kirima returned the laugh.

Then, with Cikuq leading the way through the evening twilight, Kirima grew silent. The thunderstick. The hole in the bear's skull. These thoughts pushed his triumph over Nanuq from his mind as Kirima recalled the shaman's prophecy.

These men have powerful harpoons that sound like the sea ice breaking up in the spring. Their noise echoes across the water as far as the white bear can swim. These fearsome harpoons could leave holes the size of ptarmigan eggs in the whales and seals.

Kirima sat upright in the sled bag, startled by a sudden insight. The whales and seals! The Cloud Men! Their *umiaks* did not block the path of the seals to the land. No, their terrible thundersticks killed the whales, the walruses, and the ringed seals.

The Kabloonas, who could hunt from the distance of more than ten sled lengths, perhaps more than twenty, were responsible.

No broken taboo had brought these men to Inuit shores. The wrath of the goddess had not brought them. Nor was it simple bad luck. The whales themselves and the seal and the walrus drew the Cloud Men to the land of the People. And the Cloud Men came and slaughtered and did not honor the spirits of those they slaughtered. It was the Cloud Men who killed most of the sea animals. It was they. The Cloud Men had taken away the livelihood of the People.

Stunned by this revelation, Kirima stared across the great expanse of his homeland. Here he had been born. Here, too, he would die. And, spirits willing, his People would go on after him as he had come after those who had gone before. What would become of his People if the Cloud Men returned?

Kirima thought about luck. He thought about courage. He thought about responsibility. Then his eyes widened. Luck had not caused him to stand strong when the bear charged. Luck had not caused him to stand bravely until his spear had penetrated the great bear's breast. No, it was not luck. He, Kirima, alone on the ice, had vanquished his fear and triumphed. And he, Kirima, could no longer blame bad luck or other people. He alone bore responsibility for his actions, just as the Cloud Men bore responsibility for theirs.

Father, I can feel your spirit looking down at me with pride.

When the dogs had traveled the length of their sled many times over, Kirima looked back toward the darkening horizon. Calling to his team, Kirima slowed the dogs to a walk; they could follow the scent of Cikuq's sled as easily as they could track the aboveground path of the lemming. The evening light dimmed, and the sky seemed to turn the color of deep sea water.

As if by magic, the young man heard the shaman's words speaking in his ear. The voice was deep and resonant as it reverberated inside Kirima's mind. "A great change has come upon the People," he murmured, repeating Angakok's prophecy out loud.

Kirima leaned back against the side of the sled basket and thought about the coming of the Cloud Men to his people's shores. *The white hunters of the* umiak *have not seen the last of our shores. Where the whales swim, where the seals dive, the Cloud Men will visit again, just as the People find their way back to rich hunting grounds. The Cloud Men will return with their thundersticks and their anger. They will change the way of the Inuit forever.*

How would his village meet that challenge in times to come? Would the Cloud Men play as big a role in the future of the People as Kirima himself had played in the life of one white man these past many days?

Would he ever see Cloud Man again?

Kirima shook his head, returning his attention to the sounds of his dogs' panting and the creak of their harnesses. Cikuq was a short distance ahead, seemingly asleep on the back of his sled as his dogs, walking now, broke the trail for them both.

That man can sleep anywhere!

But Kirima remained too agitated to rest. He wanted to be home with news of his adventures. He wanted to voice his fears for his people.

He rehearsed the description of the man with skin the color of the clouds. He puzzled over how to accurately describe the Cloud Men's angry character and their inability to hide their emotions. He pondered the Cloud Men's generosity and ability to cooperate as well. Perhaps these Cloud Men were indeed very similar to Inuit children.

Then Kirima smiled a small, secret smile and allowed himself a few minutes of bravado. He would tell the story of the white bear with downcast eyes and few words, but its impact would be great. He would describe how high the bear rose as he, Kirima, waited only an arm's length away, braced for the attack. He would tell how he stood strong and still. He would imitate the loud crack of his spear as the bear's weight shattered the shaft of the weapon and the bear crashed to the ice. He would mimic the boom of the thunderstick and describe the egg-sized hole in the bear's skull.

How Apak would smile with delight at his grandson's bravery. How overjoyed Grandmother would be when Kirima arrived with a bearskin large enough to make two pairs of winter trousers. How happy the villagers would be to share his new knife, one sharper and more finely crafted than any in the winter camp.

The shaman would be proud to learn that Kirima had fulfilled his destiny. Baral would rejoice at the return of the seal. Oki would take his face between her hands and sniff his nose with affection. The villagers would be astounded to see and touch the bod-dul. He pictured his grandmother's amazement at the account of his journey, even though he brought back no seal meat for her cooking pot. He would present her with the bod-dul as a sign of respect.

And Yutu! How the bully would envy him. Yutu, who owned no dogs and had no wife. Yutu, who had neither fought the mighty bear, nor even ventured out on his own, was still a boy. Yutu would never dare to torment Kirima again.

And Kirima might even lead the men of the winter camp back to the crushed *umiak* to show them the wonders of the tall antlers and the wooden hull. If the crushed boat had indeed been abandoned, perhaps he could venture onto its wooden planks and find one more of the precious knives!

Kirima would return to the village with a new look in his eye, a new carriage to his body. He would never again be told to chink snow into *iglu* walls, nor would he endure the endless recitations of the lessons learned during his boyhood. His head would now rule his heart, and he would stand tall and proud. He would rely on himself, not luck, to bring seals and caribou to his waiting spear. He would not blame others for his shortcomings.

Today, Kirima had triumphed. Today, in the spring of the high arctic, he had become a true man of the People. Now he was ready to take his full place as head of his family. He was ready to trade seal skins for a dog team of his own and provide for his grandfather and grandmother. Why, in time, he would claim a wife much like Liak, with laughing eyes, tiny sewing stitches, and strong teeth. Kirima was ready.

For, on this day in early spring, far from the winter seal camp he called home, Kirima had left childhood behind forever.

Glossary

Angakok shaman

Anningan Moon God

Aukaneck god who lives on land and controls the movements of the whales

Chukchi Chukchi are the Siberian inuit who created the Siberian husky sled dog. Origiinally, the King William Island Inuit were descended from the Chukchi.

Keelut evil spirit that often comes to earth as a dog

Kinak god of the north winds

Maiksuk command to sled team

Malina Sun Goddess

nangminarit collective term for seal partners

Nanuq polar bear, usage restricted to Kirima's mortal enemy

Netsilik People of the Seal

Nunam Earth Goddess

oitsualik puff grass

okpat hindquarter partner

oomingmak musk oxen

pana snow knife

pilaut all-purpose knife

qetrar sharp ice crust

qiviut undercoat
Sedna Goddess of the Sea
sennerak side partner
Sila god who breathes life into us all
Sklumyoa Great Spirit
Takiyok cry of joy
Tapasuma a goddess
Tatqeq Moon Spirit
Toratsiarpok command to sled team
Ukaliq arctic hare
ulu woman's knife
umiak boat

Made in the USA
Middletown, DE
02 September 2020

16646023R00116